Under
the
Mummy's
Spell

Under the Mummy's Spell

KATE McMULLAN

FARRAR / STRAUS / GIROUX · *New York*

For Wes Adams

Under
the
Mummy's
Spell

1

FROM INSIDE THE PRISON, HARRING THE DARING HEARD the demented laughter of the Lizard Warrior.

"No one has ever escaped from our chamber of horrors!" cried the scaly fiend. "I dare you to try! I dare you!"

Dare! The familiar thrill of challenge ran down Harring's spine. He could see that the walls of his square, windowless cell were closing in. His only hope of not being squashed between them like an insect lay in the seam that ran between the cell's double stainless-steel doors. Reaching to his secret leg holster for his Ninja sai, Harring turned his back to the seam. He closed his eyes and uttered his power mantra: "Hiiy-yah!" Raising his weapon, he spun on his heel and brought it down. It was working! The seam was widening, opening, splitting the panels apart . . .

"Good heavens, Peter! Watch what you're doing with that football!" Mrs. Lathrop from the fifth floor stepped into the elevator, positioning herself as far as possible from the offending boy with the fiery red hair.

"Sorry," Peter muttered.

The two passengers descended in silence to the lobby of the apartment building, where once again the seam in the stainless-steel panel parted.

Peter followed Mrs. Lathrop out of the elevator, spotting Rodent, tall and lean, slouching against the doorman's desk along the opposite wall like some low-level gangster's errand boy. He also caught a glimpse of himself in the mirrored lobby wall and winced. Harring the Daring was, in fact, not a figure of heroic proportions. When the school nurse, old Miss Feigenbaum, had taken the annual height-and-weight measurements at P.S. 40 last spring, Peter remembered her snorting as he stepped up on the scale. "You're about due for a growth spurt, aren't you, Harring?" she'd barked out, so that anyone with ears could hear. But she was right. Every girl in his sixth-grade class last year seemed to have him beat by at least two inches, not to mention ten pounds.

"Took you long enough," said Rodent. "Let's go."

Since their summer soccer league had ended, Peter and Rodent were keeping each other out of trouble for the two weeks until school began again. Peter's mother had set strict boundaries for where they could go in the city, and Madison Square Park was just about the only place of interest within them.

Rodent started to open the glass lobby door, then stopped. "Aw, Howie and his pals are out there."

"Not again!"

Rodent sighed. "You don't have to keep taking his stupid dares, you know."

"Harring the Daring never welshes on a dare." Peter ran his tongue over his chipped front tooth, the result of not welshing on a dare to eat a dog biscuit.

"Right," said Rodent. "But maybe it's time to start."

Peter peered through the glass at Howie, standing on the corner between two brutish attendants, waiting for Peter to come outside so that he could have some fun. As he waited, he rolled his skateboard back and forth on the sidewalk beneath what Peter estimated was at least a size 14 sneaker.

Last week this veritable hulk had socked Peter in the nose. Hard. The swelling had gone down and the purple bruise had faded to a sickly yellow, but still, Peter didn't think his nose could stand a second punch. One, in his opinion, was enough to pay for his crime.

How he wished that he and Charlie Bemmelmann had never seen Coach Kelly's alphabetized list on the last day of summer soccer. Then they never would have noticed the name *Krieger, Howard Hilary* and Charlie never would have dared him and he never would have called out: "Oh, yoo-hoo! Howie! Howie *Hilary!*"

This, unfortunately, got Howie's attention. Shoving a small boy out of his way, he began walking toward Peter. He seemed to move in slow motion, and Peter began to observe certain disturbing things about him. Howard Hilary Krieger was big. Much bigger than Peter had ever realized. His forehead was flat and it sloped severely back from his milky-blue eyes to his greasy yellow hair. His body seemed to be made of one large flexed muscle.

"Hey! Just a joke, Howie!" Peter jabbered as he

backed up. "We all got middle names, you know? You can't help what your parents picked."

Howie raised his upper lip in a sneer and kept on coming.

"I'll tell you my middle name, okay? Okay?" Peter backed up some more. "It's uh . . . Elizabeth. No kidding. Peter Elizabeth Harring."

The juggernaut advanced.

"It was a dare!" cried Peter desperately. "I had to do it."

"Yeah?" Howie's voice was gravelly. "Somebody dares you, you do it?"

"Sure." Peter shrugged. "You know, Harring the Daring?"

"Okay, Harring the Daring, I dare you to punch me in the nose."

"Hey, no. I don't want to fight."

"I dare you." Howie smiled, revealing jagged teeth.

What choice did Peter have? He made a feeble fist and wobbled it in the direction of Howie's face. As his knuckles glanced Howie's chin, he saw his new-found foe double up his hand. The next thing he knew, he was sitting on hard asphalt, with blood from his nose dripping steadily onto his T-shirt.

Howard Hilary Krieger stood above him. "Self-defense," he claimed. Then he leered at his two beefy stooges. "Maybe the rest of the summer won't be so boring after all, guys. Not with Harring the Daring around."

Now, with Howie lurking outside his building, Peter felt trapped. He wondered if he and Rodent shouldn't give up going to the park and retreat to his apartment to watch TV. The soaps would certainly be more entertaining than another bloody nose.

"So, what are you going to do?" Rodent asked. "Spend the rest of the summer hiding out?"

Before Peter had a chance to answer, a figure loomed suddenly on the other side of the glass. He scooted back and barely missed getting his nose flattened by his own mother as she pushed open the lobby door.

"What are you doing here, Mom?"

"I told you this morning, Peter. Bookworld gave me the day off. Your sister forgot the lunch I packed for the field trip she's taking with the Junior Scientists, so I ran it down to the camp and stopped by here to check the mail before I go uptown." Mrs. Harring pushed a strand of her dark hair from her face. "Hi, Rode," she added.

Most adults, Rodent had found, were unable to address him by the name of a rather unappealing, gnawing vermin. They didn't seem to object to calling him Rode, however, which perhaps allowed them to pretend that it was short for Rodney or Roderick. But with his small, dark eyes, big teeth, prominent nose, and less than prominent chin, Rodent had figured out early in life that some wise guys were going to start calling him Ratface some day, so he'd decided to give himself a nickname on his own terms. His mother had named him Alexander Calder Potts, after a favorite sculptor, but she alone now called him Alex.

"Hi, Mrs. H.," said Rodent.

"You boys on your way to the park?"

Peter shrugged.

"I'm about to go up to the Met. They have a new exhibit of Chinese porcelains from the Han Dynasty, and— Say, why don't you two come with me?"

"Not a chance, Mom."

"Oh, come on! You'd like to, wouldn't you, Rode?"

"It's okay by me." Actually, Rodent would have toured the New York City sewer system if Mrs. Harring had suggested it. She was a real *mom*, a cookie baker, hot-chocolate maker, mender of holey socks. A kiss-'em-and-tuck-'em-into-bed-at-night mom. Not like Lucinda, not some weirdo artist who just happened to have a son. The only time she ever used the oven was to fire a piece of pottery. No wonder his dad had packed a suitcase five years ago and taken off for Los Angeles. Rodent hadn't seen him since.

"Don't be so stubborn, Peter," Mrs. Harring was saying.

Out on the sidewalk, Peter caught another glimpse of the waiting Howie, whose T-shirt was chopped off to showcase his rippling stomach muscles. "You know," he said, "I always like to check out the mummies at the Met."

"Do come! A little exposure to art won't hurt you!"

Later, much later, after things had calmed down again, Peter remembered her saying this. It just went to prove that mothers aren't always right. And in this case, his mother couldn't have been more wrong.

Egypt, Year XVI of the Reign of Pharaoh Amenhut

The leopard-coated cat Khaibit crouched against the mud-brick stable wall as Nephia—his own girl!—stroked the neck of the wild white stallion. He pretended not to see as she wedged one bare foot into a chink in the brick and stepped up, whispering tenderly to the horse as slowly, slowly she worked her fingers into its mane. Grasping tightly, she pushed off from the wall, swinging one leg over the horse's broad back. Her dozen long, thin braids bounced against her shoulders and she was on! The horse took a few steps back, raised its head and whinnied. On the ground below, Khaibit shut his eyes against the four formidable hooves stomping so rudely in the dust.

Several servants of the Royal Stable clicked their tongues in dismay as they saw the dirt-streaked Princess, daughter of the God-King Pharaoh Amenhut, seated like a common soldier on the back of a horse.

Nephia gripped hard with her knees. Pulling gently on its mane, she steered the stallion out the stable gate and immediately dug in with her heels, asking for speed. Off the two galloped, more swiftly than the desert wind.

From a palace window, a pair of eyes outlined in black followed Nephia as she rode into the distance. These were the eyes of Tachu, elder sister to the Pharaoh. Tachu ran her fingers lightly over the head of the slim, green snake coiled at her wrist. Horrid Nephia! Ever stinking of the stable! Always bubbling with happiness; it was enough to turn one's stomach! Yet, these days, Tachu thought, it was easier to forgive this bothersome girl, for she had provided the perfect inspiration for her scheme to rule Egypt!

Not until Nephia was a mere speck on the horizon did Tachu step away from the window. Grasping her cold-blooded pet by the throat, she forced open its mouth. Poison glistened from two pinpoint fangs. Quickly, Tachu reached for a bowl covered tightly with linen and pressed the snake's top jaw down on it. The fangs pierced the cloth, and with a steady stroke Tachu milked the little viper of its golden venom. A single drop in a goblet of wine, she had found years ago, could induce a raging fever in a servant girl; twin drops could stop the heart of the most robust galley slave.

Back in the stable yard, Khaibit yawned and gave his left front leg two annoyed licks. Then he sauntered along the wall, rubbing his chin against its corners, marking each one with his own strong and satisfying scent. He would find a safe place, far from any disorderly hooves, to curl up and wait for his girl to come home. He was rarely separated from Nephia, but when he was, the only solution was a nap.

2

PETER AND RODENT TOOK THE STEPS TWO AT A time out of the Eighty-sixth Street subway stop. After a forced detour to Junque, Inc., a thrift shop where Peter's mother bought a beaded evening bag, the trio hiked across town and joined the hordes of August tourists walking up the stone steps and into the Great Hall of the Metropolitan Museum of Art.

At the admission booth, Mrs. Harring offered a twenty-dollar bill. "One adult, please," she said. "And three dollars each for the boys."

"Hey, Peter, you could probably still make it in for free," said Rodent, pointing to the sign that read CHILDREN UNDER TWELVE, NO ADMISSION FEE.

"Thanks a heap."

As they each clipped a blue tin admission button to their shirts, Mrs. Harring outlined her itinerary. "Let's visit the Chinese exhibit first and then the European paintings."

"But we just want to check out the knights and the mummies," objected Peter. He and Rodent walked by the guard at the west entrance, tilting their heads so that their MMA buttons showed.

"Oh, for goodness' sakes, Peter, it's time you broadened your horizons." Mrs. Harring started to pass by the guard, but he held up a hand.

"You'll have to check your shopping bag, ma'am."

"This? It's nothing." Mrs. Harring opened the thrift-shop bag for the guard. "Isn't the beadwork exquisite?"

"I'm sure it is, but no parcels of any size are allowed in the museum."

Mrs. Harring turned toward the line at the check booth.

"See you, Mom!" Peter waved the folded floor plan he'd picked up. "We'll meet you later, just name the spot."

"All right, all right. It's two-thirty now. Meet me by the information booth at four sharp."

Free at last, Peter and Rodent headed for the large, dimly lit gallery where dozens of suits of armor stood posed as if invisible knights inside were ready for battle. Peter stopped next to his favorite, a silvery suit in the corner, exactly his height. He always liked to be reminded that in days of old there had been a real, live knight who was just as short as he was. The helmet was sleek and sinister, with a narrow slit at eye level and a pointed metal beak to protect the nose. Peter wished he could be wearing this helmet the next time he ran into Howie Krieger . . .

"O worshipful warrior," spake the King, "never have I had so great a need of a knight's help."

"My liege," spake Sir Harring de Daring, "I shall take the battle for you."

"Yet you ask not the name of thine opponent," spake the King. "It is none other than the varlet Howard de Hulk."

"I fear not, my liege." Sir Harring in his armor full mounted his steed and took him up his spear, and in the presence of kings, judges, and knights did he gallop toward de Hulk. On a worthy charger came de Hulk, and the two mighty spears clashed together like thunder, but through great strength did Sir Harring strike the varlet down!

Then did Sir Harring alight from his steed to the great cheering of the crowds and . . .

"Nice helmet." Rodent slid up next to Peter. "But enough of these tin cans. Let's go find the mummies."

Reluctantly leaving the knight, Peter led Rodent through long hallways lined with antique furniture. They entered a vast gallery with a wall made of windows that slanted in as it neared the ceiling high above. In the center of the room, a huge elevated platform supported a stone gateway and temple. A shallow pool, its bottom dotted with coins, formed a U-shape around one narrow side of the platform.

"The Temple of Dendur," mused Peter. "Remember?"

"Brought over stone by stone from beside the Nile," Rodent said in his celebrated imitation of their third-grade teacher, Ms. McCoy. "You got any change?"

Peter dug into his pants pocket and came up with a dime, a penny, and a stale stick of gum. He offered up the penny, but his pal filched the dime. Humming the first few bars of "California, Here I Come," Rodent flipped the coin off his thumb and it somersaulted into the pool.

Peter balanced the penny on the back of his hand. He could wish for plenty of things. That Howie Krieger would be kidnapped by aliens. That his little sister would be struck mute. Or that the growth spurt predicted by old Miss Feigenbaum would start.

"Spit it out, Pete."

Peter shrugged and tossed his penny.

"I wish something would happen."

IN THE DEAD OF NIGHT, PHARAOH AMENHUT'S HEART pounded with fear. But fear of what? He knew not. He knew only that a feeling of great dread had come upon him as he lay in the dark waiting for sleep, and he could summon no soothing thoughts to banish it.

There was no reason to be fearful. The Pharaoh had called his armies home from the lands beyond the desert, for at last his country was at peace. The Nile had flooded on schedule this year, coating Egypt's soil with its rich, black silt. Crops would be plentiful; no one would go hungry. In fact, he had every reason to fall into a most contented sleep, for tonight he had finally finished the poem he had been struggling with since the new moon.

What, then, could be causing his heart to gallop like that brash white stallion on whose back his only daughter seemed to spend her every waking moment? The Pharaoh frowned. Why Nephia doted on this snorting beast was a mystery to him. As he thought of her, his dread grew stronger. Something was wrong, he could feel it. Perhaps she was ill, hurt . . .

Throwing back his covers and taking up a lamp, the Pharaoh hurried from his chamber. His bare feet made no sound as he rushed along the cool stone floors of the palace hallways. Outside his daughter's room, Amenhut nodded to a sleepy servant and entered the chamber.

There on her golden bed lay Nephia, his lovely girl. He saw the rise and fall of her steady breathing as she slept soundly in the warm night. Of course Nephia was safe. He had been foolish to worry.

In the lamplight, the contours of Nephia's face reminded the Pharaoh sharply of his beloved wife, Hapii—*Osiris, bless her star-spirit shining in the sky!* Yes, Nephia was a young woman now. In one more day, she would finish her twelfth year. But, Amenhut knew, she would not be too old to turn cartwheels of joy when she discovered that, in honor of her birthday, Tachu had planned a chariot race. Tachu, his own sister! Did she not know better than to encourage Nephia in this horse frenzy of hers? How he wished the Hyksos had never ridden their fly-bitten beasts into the Land of Egypt!

Thinking of horses, the Pharaoh frowned once more, and then a small smile softened his lips. He never could have kept his secret from Hapii, his childhood playmate, his half-sister, his wife since his own twelfth year. Certainly she would have guessed why he kept his distance from the Royal Stables. How odd that he, who was worshipped as a god, trembled at the sight of a horse!

Stirred by a dream, Nephia mumbled and turned, and Amenhut saw that, even in sleep, Khaibit was by her side. His head rested on Nephia's shoulder and her arm encircled him. The cat opened one green eye and studied the Pharaoh. Then he closed it again.

How well Amenhut remembered the night six years ago when the spotted cat first wandered, uninvited, into the palace; the night his dear Hapii had died of the mysterious fever. To the shock of everyone in the chamber, the cat had leapt boldly onto the Queen's bed and lay upon her chest as she took her final breath. Then it jumped down and, with its tail pointing straight up, walked directly to Nephia, purring loudly, and rubbed against her legs. The priests in attendance at the death of the Great Royal Wife informed the stunned Pharaoh that one of Hapii's seven spirits had passed into the body of the cat. They named it Khaibit, meaning "shadow-spirit."

The sight of Nephia sleeping peacefully stilled the Pharaoh's fearful heart. He kissed his daughter's cheek and tiptoed from her side.

As Amenhut walked back to his bedchamber, a new poem began to take shape in his mind; a poem about Nephia and her Spirit-cat, who, like a shadow, was always at her heels.

Far down the hallway, Amenhut spied a flickering light. Ah, Tachu, creature of the night! Was she yet awake? Amenhut had instructed her to cease her night-time ways, to snuff out the scents of sorcery that wafted from her chamber. Oh, yes, he had heard the ugly rumors of her dark magic, but at these he only scoffed. Tachu was merely obsessed with staying young and beautiful, that was all. Amenhut believed his sister spent the moonlit hours concocting strange brews—potions for inducing restful sleep, salves for eliminating wrinkles, elixirs for recapturing her youth. Why could she not heed the old saying?

Make the most of time,
For life is but a dream
And all must die.

The Pharaoh thought of stopping by Tachu's room, but he would only scold, and the new poem was spinning in his head. He wanted to write it down while it was fresh, before he lost it, and so he hurried on.

3

"CHARLIE TOLD ME THERE'S A MUMMY HERE with his toe sticking right out of the bandages," Peter said as he pushed open a pair of tall glass doors.

"You mean with skin still on?"

"Yeah. Charlie said it looked like a piece of dried-up ham."

Peter led the way down a long hallway. But just as he was about to turn a corner, Rodent called him back.

"Check this guy," he said, crooking his thumb at a cat statue. Stenciled writing on the glass case told them that it was a coffin for a sacred cat. "He could be Guido's twin."

"Wishful thinking, Rode. Guido was a scarred-up tough guy and this cat's got on earrings. Can you picture Guido with earrings?"

"Nah, but Guido had those same big eyes." Rodent

sighed. "Killer's a great kitten and all, but he's no Guido."

"I miss him, too." Peter's parents always said *Absolutely not* whenever he begged for a cat or a dog or even a guppy, so Peter had come to love Rodent's fat old gray cat as the closest he'd ever get to a pet of his own. When Guido had died last year, Peter was just as broken up about it as Rodent. "You know, I bet I could send Guido's spirit a message through this cat."

"He was *my* cat. I should send him the message." Rodent scratched his head. "Uh, what message?"

Peter began chanting softly. "O Spirit of the Sacred Cat, come to us now and hear the words of Rodent. Send them on to the soul of his dearly departed Guido."

"I talk to him now?"

Peter nodded solemnly.

"Hey, Guido," Rodent whispered. "It's me! How's it going up there in cat heaven, huh? You got somebody to scratch your belly the way I used to do?"

As he listened, Peter felt a little breeze tickling the hairs on the back of his neck. Maybe that meant Guido's spirit was receiving the message! He turned around, but found himself nose to nose with a short, stocky woman wearing earphones. She was taking a recorded tour of the gallery and her eyes were focused on the case beyond.

Peter nudged Rodent to move on.

"Ten-four for now, Guido."

The boys wandered through hallways filled with Egyptian jewelry, Egyptian pottery, and dioramas of

Egyptian life, searching for the mummy's toe. But as they approached a promising gallery with caskets on display, they found its entrance blocked by a velvet rope and a small sign proclaiming:

GALLERY TEMPORARILY CLOSED
FOR CLEANING OF THE EXHIBITS
Guided Tours Only

"Rats," said Rodent.

Inside, the big glass cases which usually covered the mummy coffins had been removed.

"This could be our chance to take a *really* close look at the mummy's toe," whispered Peter, "if only we could get in there."

At that moment, a woman who was obviously a museum guide and a man with thick, Mr. Rogers eyebrows and a bright orange CAMP CULTURE T-shirt marched up to the gallery. Beckoning to a group of about two dozen kids, the man slid aside the pole that held one end of the velvet rope so that his campers could pass into the room. Peter nodded to Rodent and without speaking they oozed their way to the center of the pack.

Inside, eyebrow-man tried to count heads, but gave up and nodded wearily to the guide. She gathered the campers beside the first mummy case in the room, which rested on a low platform. Its sides were rounded and narrow, just big enough to cradle a body. On the top of the case, a woman's face and figure had been painted.

"This is the mummy case of Tachu," the guide began. "We know little about her life except that she was the sister of a pharaoh. In Egypt, when embalmers made a mummy, they always removed the corpse's internal organs so they didn't rot and cause the body to decay, but rumor has it that Tachu's body was perfectly preserved *whole*. No one knows if this is true or not, because Tachu's body mysteriously vanished from the museum and has never been found.''

''Her face gives me the willies,'' whispered Rodent.

The guide pointed out a large eye painted on the side of Tachu's coffin.

''According to legend, Horus, a sun-god, fought against his evil uncle, Set, ruler of darkness, for the throne of Egypt. In the battle, Set tore out Horus' left eye, but later it was magically restored. In time, this eye became a symbol of protection and the ancient Egyptians believed that the spirits of the dead were able to see into this world through the Eye of Horus. The bodies of the dead were always placed on their sides in their coffins, so they could look out through the Eye.''

''But check out *her* eyes!'' said Rodent.

Peter saw what he meant. Tachu's wide brown eyes tilted upward and were rimmed in black lines that extended toward the sides of her face. A small green dot at the inside corner of each one gave Tachu's stare a hard malevolence.

''She's giving you the evil eye,'' Peter whispered back. ''Want to send her spirit a message?''

''Naah. I wouldn't mess around with this one.''

''Because of the amulets and the magical spells written inside her coffin, some experts believe that Tachu may have been some kind of sorceress.'' The guide led them past other cases, pausing at each one to comment briefly on the portrait that an ancient artist had painted of the mummified person. Peter and Rodent were careful to examine the foot end of each case but found no protruding toes.

Beside a coffin with the wings of a spectacular bird painted on its front, a girl with glasses raised her hand. "Why did the Egyptians make mummies, anyway?"

"The ancient Egyptians believed they would need their physical bodies in the afterlife. On burial day they performed ceremonies over a mummy to create a *sahu*, or spirit body. They believed the *sahu* lived in the heavenly Land of the Dead with the gods but that it often came back to this world for a visit. The mummy provided an earthly dwelling place for the *sahu*. If the mummy was destroyed, the *sahu*, too, would die, and then that person would have no eternal life." The guide walked over to stand between two whispering culture campers. "The Egyptians believed that seven spirits lived inside the *sahu*. The most important was the *ba*, or soul." She began counting on her fingers. "Then there was the *ab*, or heart, the fountain of all thought, both good and evil; the *ren*, or the mummy's secret name; the *sekhem* spirit, or the mummy's power; the *khu*, or intelligence; the *khaibit*, or shadow-spirit—and let's see, that's six . . . oh, I left out the *ka* spirit. The *ka* was thought to be the identical twin of the dead person."

She pointed to a painting on a large section of stone hanging on the gallery wall. It showed loaves of bread, roasted birds and fish, and flagons of wine. "The Egyptians painted pictures like these on the tomb walls and believed that, by their offering prayers to the gods, the paintings magically turned into food that would nourish the *sahu* of their dead loved one when it came back to the Land of the Living. Priests and family members of the deceased also brought food to the temples and offered it to the seven spirits.''

Peter ran his tongue along his chipped tooth as he stared at the coffin. What if you really did have a spirit who would come back to visit you, but only if you had your body ready and waiting? What if, someday, Howie punched his lights out for good? Maybe he should leave a note in his desk drawer just in case, asking to be mummified . . .

Through the Eye of Horus, Harring the Daring saw his mother dabbing her eyes with a handkerchief.

''Do you think our dear Peter would like his mummy case next to the piano?'' she said, sniveling.

''Or how about here, by the window?'' Peter's father answered in a shaky voice. ''We can turn him, just slightly, so he can see out.''

''Oh, he did always love this view!'' Sobbing loudly, Peter's mother turned to Erin. ''It will be your job to make sure your brother's spirits have enough to eat and drink.''

''Oh, I will! I will!'' cried Erin, her eyes red and swollen from crying. ''Why, tonight, with my own allowance, I'll buy him a whole Ray's pizza with double cheese and sausage and pepperoni and . . .''

''This way!'' The guide began herding the group into a cramped passageway off the main room. His stomach growling, Peter stumbled along with the others as the guide pointed out a collection of carved scarabs and hundreds of miniature dolls, which were believed to become the servants of the dead in the next life.

Then they stepped out of the passageway and into a far corner of the gallery, stopping beside a small coffin. On one side of the casket was the Eye of Horus and on its lid was a painting of a girl.

Paintings had never had much effect on Peter, and neither had girls, but now the face of this girl gave him a pang of . . . what? Regret, perhaps, that she had lived and died before his time? It was a pang, at any rate, not unlike the one he'd felt when he heard that old Guido had died. As he gazed down at the small, mysterious face, Peter felt another breeze tickle the back of his neck. He turned around, but this time there was no one behind him.

In his room once more, Amenhut seated himself at his writing table. He selected a new reed pen and dipped it into the ink. But as he started to compose his poem about Nephia and Khaibit, his hand began to quiver. Strange words began to fly from beneath his pen! They appeared on the papyrus, line after line. The startled Pharaoh could only watch as his hand raced to transcribe a wondrous message.

At last, Amenhut put down his pen and wiped the perspiration from his brow. There could be no doubt of it. He had received a prophecy from Maat, goddess of justice and truth. For surely *this* was not the poem he had set out to write:

Three thousand years
shall slip away
like grains of sand
in an hourglass.

Kingdoms swollen with power
shall disappear
like morning mist
upon the Nile.

Then shall Maat send one to fight against darkness,
To battle Set's forces of evil and woe
That spilled blood for power,
That sang spells forbidden,
That plundered the tomb of an innocent soul.

Hear, Osiris,
The Seven Spirits of the Wronged One speak:

Ab, *the heart:*   Who is there to help us?

Maat: *A man of the future.*

Ba, *the soul:*   When shall he come?

Maat: *'Twixt new moon and full.*

Ren, *the secret name:*   Will any oppose him?

Maat: *An Old One is waiting.*

Sekhem, *the power:*   How can we protect him?

Maat: *Send one to stand by him.*

Khu, *the intelligence:*   How shall he know us?

Maat:	*Speak thrice; he shall hear.*
Khaibit, *the shadow:*	How shall we know him?
Maat:	*He shall give you a sign.*
Ka, *the twin:*	What sign shall he give?
Maat:	*A kiss.*

4

"Not many mummified bodies are here in the Egyptian Galleries," the guide informed them. "You see, this is an art museum. The paintings on the cases are works of art, but we often send the actual mummies over to the Museum of Natural History."

"That's a dirty deal," Peter muttered.

"But let me introduce you," said the guide, gesturing toward the small coffin, "to Princess Nephia. She was the only daughter of Pharaoh Amenhut and her mummy lies undisturbed inside this case. She was just twelve years old when she died."

I'm twelve, thought Peter.

"We know this because Nephia's father wrote many touching poems about her and his scrolls were found inside her tomb."

"How did she die?" asked a girl.

"From what we can understand of Amenhut's writing, she died in a riding accident."

A boy wearing a Yankees T-shirt raised his hand. "Why wasn't her mummy taken out like the rest?"

"The lid of Nephia's mummy case is tightly sealed to the base," the guide explained. "The curators here did not want to risk damaging the exquisite paintings on the outside by forcing it, so the coffin has never been opened, not in more than three thousand years."

The guide motioned the group closer, waiting until they had all pressed around, and then she pointed to a band about eight inches high along one side of the coffin. "This painting depicts Nephia's funeral procession, which has reached the tomb site. Her mummy is being held upright for the Opening of the Mouth ceremony in which a priest touched a wand to her mouth, eyes, and ears. This ritual was supposed to give the mummy the power to speak, see, hear, and move about in the Land of the Dead." The guide slid her finger along the casket. "This is the Pharaoh, Nephia's father, kneeling at her feet. His hand is shown over his head like that because he is throwing dust on himself. This is how people in ancient Egypt mourned."

Indicating a line of men walking in profile wearing short white kilts, she added, "These are servants bearing gifts for Princess Nephia's spirits to enjoy in the next life." The parade marched all the way around to the Eye of Horus on the other side of the mummy case, each servant carrying on his shoulders a golden statue or a jewelry box, a fancy bed or a basket of fruit, a loaf of bread or even a whole oxen.

"Check it out!"

"Yeah," said Peter. "Makes me hungry."

"I don't mean the food," scoffed Rodent. "Check out the gold! The jewels! This was one rich twelve-year-old kid."

The guide pointed to a figure at the very end of the procession, a woman in a tight-fitting red garment. "Some experts believe this is Nephia's aunt, Tachu, whose mummy case we saw first in this gallery."

"Old Evil Eyes," whispered Peter.

"But no one can explain why she is at the end of the procession rather than at the front with her brother."

The guide swept her hand along the top of the casket. "The painting on the lid of Nephia's mummy case is one of the most unusual ever discovered. Can anyone guess why?"

Peter thought maybe it was Nephia's lips, the way they turned up ever so slightly in a half-sad smile. Or her eyes, which were not at all scary, not like that other mummy's. No, Nephia's gaze was steady and proud, the way a princess's should be. In fact, she seemed to look right out at him, as if she knew some remarkable secret she could hardly keep from telling.

"Is she holding a doll?" asked a camper.

"Not a doll," said the guide.

Peter barely made out a small, golden head with pointed ears. Eyes like green marbles peeked out from behind Nephia's arms.

"She's got a cat."

Thick eyebrows went up as the Camp Culture leader tried to place this scrawny redhead, but the guide went on talking.

"That's right, a cat. In several scrolls, Amenhut wrote of a cat named Khaibit, after the shadow spirit, that Nephia loved dearly. One particularly fine poem tells how Khaibit always stuck as close to Nephia as her shadow." The guide stepped away from the casket. "Are there any questions?"

No hands went up.

"Then follow me, please." Her high heels clicked on the pink marble floor. "And on your way, be sure to take a look at the beautifully carved head of Pharaoh Amenhut."

Even though the Pharaoh's face was no more than cold carved stone, Peter thought that the sculptor had managed to make him appear careworn yet kind.

"In this gallery," the guide continued from the next room, "are the great Sphinx statues of Hatshepsut. When she was a young woman, Hatshepsut claimed that a god visited her and said, 'Go, my daughter, be king!' So she strapped a golden beard to her chin and reigned as Pharaoh of Egypt for more than twenty years."

Rodent started to move into the next gallery along with the group, but Peter grabbed his shirt and pulled him over into the narrow passage. "Wait," he whispered. "We have to find that mummy's toe. It's got to be in this room."

"But the guards, they'll see us."

"Shhhh!"

The culture campers straggled off. At last the boys were alone in the gallery.

"Gives me the creeps in here," Rodent whispered.

Keeping low, Peter led the way out from their hiding

place. They reinspected each pair of mummy feet but saw no toes. Finally, they came once more to Princess Nephia's coffin.

"You ever been this close to a real mummy, Rodent?"

"I don't think so."

"You don't *think* so?"

"No," he admitted. "I never have."

"We could touch this one."

"Something tells me not to, Pete. I got a real strong feeling not to."

"It's no big a deal."

"No?" Rodent bristled. "Okay, you touch it then. Go ahead. I dare you."

A smile formed on the lips of Harring the Daring. "It's just her coffin, but still, her mummy's right inside." He stepped closer.

"Hold it a sec, Pete," began Rodent. "Maybe you shouldn't . . ."

But Peter had already slipped around to the other side of Nephia's casket. He swiveled his head, checking for guards, and seeing none, bent down swiftly and gave the princess's painted face a kiss.

WHEN AMENHUT FIRST SHOWED TACHU THE MYSTERIOUS prophecy from Maat, she was puzzled. Yet something about it intrigued her. She asked the Pharaoh to copy it out for her so that she might take time to consider its meaning. Over and over she had read it, some gibberish about a man of the future, but she could make no sense of it. So she rolled up the papyrus and tucked it away. For the present, she had more important matters on her mind.

Tachu chanted softly to Set, god of night, as she sat before her mirror of polished bronze. She straightened her best blue wig, steadied her cobra headdress. The chariot driver she was meeting at midnight must understand what a powerful woman she was; must understand that it was too late for him to back out now.

Carefully, Tachu selected a thin brush and began painting a dark line of kohl on the upper lid of one eye. Thank Set that her brother had no male children, no clear heir to the throne. And, should some catastrophe befall him, who was a closer blood relative than the Pharaoh's sister? Tachu turned her attention to painting the other eye. Ah, this plan of hers had taken many dark nights to perfect. And tomorrow was the day! When it was over, no more would the Upper and Lower Kingdoms have an ostrich for a Pharaoh, hiding his head in the sands of poetry. At last Egypt would have a ruler who could command its troops; a ruler with a heart for war.

Tachu picked up a slender new brush and dipped its tip into a tiny glass bottle. At the inside corner of each eye, she placed a small green dot. Now she leaned back from the mirror to behold her handiwork. Tachu smiled. The mirror reflected her intentions. Looking back at her was a woman clearly powerful enough to sit on the throne of Egypt!

5

 As his lips brushed against nephia's mysterious smile, Peter felt a prickling in his scalp. The beating of wings echoed in his ears, followed by a deafening clap of thunder. A voice like the tinkling of wind chimes sang into his thoughts. *"O man of the future! Bring back the treasure of my soul!"*

Peter yelped and fell backward, banging his head on the case next to Nephia's, then sliding onto the cold marble floor. His heart beat frantically. He heard Rodent, but his voice sounded miles away. Gripping the princess's coffin, Peter clambered to his knees.

"You! Boys!" A guard with a slim gray mustache and an angry expression was scuttling across the gallery toward them. "What are you doing? Remove your hands from there at once!"

Rodent peeled Peter's hands off the mummy case and pulled him to a stand. "He's not feeling too good," Rodent told the guard quickly. "I think I better take him to the bathroom before he tosses his tacos all over the floor. Which way is it?''

''Down the hall, past the Temple.'' The guard pointed. ''And please, after this, stay with your group!''

''We will!'' Rodent pushed Peter to get him moving out of the gallery. ''We will!''

Peter let Rodent lead him through the tall glass doors and over to a bench beside the Temple of Dendur.

''You okay, Pete? You really knocked your head a good one.'' His friend was breathing hard. ''You got a concussion? Say something!''

''Was she t-talking to me?''

''Who?''

''Her.''

''Her who?''

Peter blinked. ''Didn't you hear what she said?''

''*Who* said?''

''You . . . you know.''

''No, I don't. I didn't hear anybody.''

''You didn't?'' Peter grabbed Rodent's arm. ''I did, Rode. I heard the *mummy*!''

''The mummy?'' Rodent wrenched away. ''What are you saying?''

Peter's eyes darted wildly. ''I did! She called me . . . something.''

''Something horrible?''

''A . . . a man of the future.''

''Oh.'' Rodent sounded disappointed.

''And, Rode! She told me to bring her a treasure.''

''Aw, you're just imagining it, like the time you thought you saw a ghost in Charlie's bathroom, remember? And it was just his sister's old slip?''

Peter shook his head. "This was real. I know I heard it. *O man of the future*"—he scowled, trying to remember—*"bring back the treasure . . . of my soul."*

"Yeah? Maybe the treasure's here, in the museum, lost in some storage room, and we could find it and—"

"Forget it, Rodent! I'm hearing mummy voices and all you can think about is getting rich!"

"You're right," Rodent agreed. "Come on. It's almost four."

Rodent guided Peter back through the Arms and Armor Gallery into the museum's Great Hall. They sat down to wait on a circular bench surrounding a planted flower bed. A few minutes later, when Mrs. Harring appeared, Peter was feeling a little calmer.

"Well, you boys are right on time. Did you get to see everything you wanted?"

"Everything," Rodent told her.

"Well, I wish you'd come with me. Those Chinese porcelains were absolutely—"

"Mom," Peter interrupted, "I don't feel so hot. Can we take a taxi home?"

"A taxi? From here, Peter? That would cost a fortune."

"Please!" begged Peter.

"Yeah, Mrs. H.! A limo would be better, but we'll settle for a taxi."

Peter's mother laughed. "Really, Rode, I believe you'd try to sell ice at the North Pole!" She picked up her bag from the check booth and the three of them headed out of the museum, dropping their MMA buttons into a big clear plastic container on the way.

But at the exit they stopped short. The blue sky of the early afternoon was now churning with an angry black thunderhead cloud. Daylight had faded to an eerie green darkness, and rain fell in sheets.

"I can't believe my eyes! There was no mention of rain in the weather report this morning." Mrs. Harring turned to Peter. "Now I wish we could find a taxi, but everybody will be after one in this downpour."

They dashed down the museum steps, pelted by the heavy rain. At least two dozen people were standing out on the sidewalk, all trying to hail a cab.

"Come on," Mrs. Harring urged. "We've got to run over to the subway."

"Wait!" said Peter. "Here comes one." He stepped out into the avenue as lightning ripped the dark sky over his head. He raised his right hand. A crack of thunder split the air. "Taxi!" he shouted over the rumble. "TAXI!"

As if out of nowhere, a big Checker cab chugged through the gloom down Fifth Avenue. Turning on its blinker, it passed by drenched women waving briefcases. It passed by sopping men in three-piece suits holding wet gray newspapers over their heads. It veered toward Peter and stopped—directly in front of him.

A MUSCULAR MAN WITH EYES AS SHIFTY AS A CROCODILE'S came to the palace gate. He pressed the scarab he had been told to use as a sign into the palm of a serving girl and, under cover of darkness, followed her down long corridors to a curtained doorway. The servant bowed and slipped away, leaving him to whisper a secret word into the stillness of the night.

The word had barely left his lips when the curtain was drawn back by a tall woman dressed in scarlet. Her eyes still frightened him, as they had after he had won the chariot race in Thebes, the first time she had spoken to him. He bowed, partly to avoid her gaze.

The sister of the Pharaoh caressed the small green snake coiled at her wrist and beckoned the chariot driver into her chamber. There, she presented him with a golden helmet. The driver accepted it with another bow. It was not the first thing he had accepted from the Pharaoh's sister.

And, thought Tachu, it would not be the last. She had promised him that, after he had done her bidding, she would find him a place in the country where he could live out the rest of his days in safety. But, in truth, the final gift that Tachu planned for her driver was a tumbler of beer to which she would add two tiny golden drops.

6

 "THIS IS SOME SORT OF MIRACLE." FENDING OFF two men who argued that they had seen the taxi first, Mrs. Harring quickly opened the door. "Hurry in, boys!"

Peter started to climb into the dim interior of the cab but stopped short. "Hey!" he cried. "There's a—"

"Peter!" exclaimed his mother. "We're getting soaked!"

"But there's a *dog* in here."

"Move it, Pete!" Rodent yelled, prodding his friend from behind.

Peter scooted cautiously across the seat, holding his feet up, and the others followed.

"Whew!" Mrs. Harring said, rain dripping off her eyebrows and nose. "Twenty-eighth and Lexington, please."

The taxi had already pulled out from the curb before she looked over at the shivering animal huddled miserably on the taxi floor. "Driver!" She knocked on the partition between the front seat and the back. "Is this any way to treat an animal?"

"What's that?"

"Your dog!"

The driver stopped for a red light and turned around. "What dog are you talking about?"

"This one!" Peter's mother pointed to the dog, which had now raised itself to a sitting position. "What do you mean by keeping this poor wet creature in here?"

As the driver craned his neck to see the dog, the cars behind him started honking and he had to turn back around. "Lady," he said as he swerved around a double-parked delivery van, "I've never seen that dog before in my life."

It was a big dog, shorthaired, with upright ears and wide yellow eyes. "Hey, puppy." Peter tentatively reached out a hand and patted its head.

"Must be raining cats and dogs, huh?" said Rodent. "Dogs, anyway."

The dog inched closer to Peter, resting its chin on his lap. It wore a metal collar; not a choke collar made of separate links, but a wide metal hoop that fit snugly around its neck. Turning the collar, Peter found a metal disk about the size of a quarter, but instead of having the name and phone number of the dog's owner inscribed on it, it had an odd oval mark. He continued stroking the dog's silky head. Somehow he felt that he had met this dog before, had known it for years instead of only a few minutes. He ached to ask if he could keep it, but he already knew the answer.

"My turn," Rodent said.

Peter leaned back so that Rodent could pet the dog's head, but the yellow eyes never left Peter's brown ones. The dog put a wet paw on Peter's leg and stopped trembling.

At the next red light, the driver turned around again and shook his head. "It's disgusting, that's what it is. Must've been that dame I just took up to Ninety-sixth Street. Never even saw her put the dog in my hack, and then she gets out and abandons it! Some people!"

"Why, that's terrible!"

Peter heard the note of outrage in his mother's voice. A good sign.

"What are you going to do with him?" Rodent asked.

"Haul him up to the pound, I guess." The driver sighed. "Dirty trick, making someone else get rid of your unwanted dog!"

Peter noticed that his mother hadn't said anything about the smudgy black paw prints all over his khakis. Another good sign. He and Rodent stroked the dog in silence as the taxi wove in and out of traffic down Fifth Avenue and then turned east on a side street.

Peter's mother reached over and patted the dog's wet head. "You got yourself good and wet, didn't you, pup?"

That was it: sign number three.

Peter cleared his throat. "Can we keep him, Mom?"

"Keep him? Oh, don't be ridiculous, Peter!"

"Say yes, Mrs. H.!" Rodent begged for his friend. "Peter'll feed him and walk him and scoop up the doggie-doo, won't you, Pete?"

"Twice a day! Three times!"

"But he's wearing a collar," said Mrs. Harring. "He belongs to someone."

The taxi pulled up to the curb just below Twenty-eighth Street. "Lady," the driver said, "you take the dog and the ride's on me. You'll save me at least an hour on the FDR Drive getting it to the pound."

"But surely this dog's owner will be trying to find it." Mrs. Harring turned to her son. "Does he have any identification?"

Peter examined the tag again. "Just some weird picture. Looks like a football with a baseball inside."

The driver scrawled something on the corner of his newspaper and tore it off. "Here's my dispatcher's phone number. Call in a couple days, and if someone wants this mutt back, there'll be a message." He put the scrap of paper through the opening in the Plexiglas divider. "But I'll bet dollars to doughnuts that there won't be any call."

"I'll take care of him, Mom. I promise!"

"Having a dog is a huge responsibility, Peter," began Mrs. Harring. "Why, most mornings, you don't even make your bed . . ."

As she spoke, the dog closed its eyes for a moment, and when it opened them, round and yellow, it was staring at Peter's mother.

". . . or hang up your towel, or . . ." Mrs. Harring looked down into the dog's eyes and stopped mid-sentence. When she spoke again, Peter could hardly believe his ears. "Well, perhaps having a pet will help you learn to be more dependable."

"You mean I can keep him?"

"At least until his rightful owners are found."

"Whoopie!" Peter wrapped both arms around the dog's neck, hugging him close, and then scooted him out of the taxi.

The driver gave Peter a two-fingered salute before pulling away from the curb.

Peter grinned. The dog standing proudly beside him on the sidewalk was a rich tan, the color of acorns, except for a white star on its chest and a white tip on its slim tail, which curled up over its rear end like the top half of a question mark. Its legs were long, its body lean and muscular. Its head came up to Peter's elbow. His dog . . . almost.

Peter turned to his mother. "Thank you! Thank you! Thank you!"

And then a voice, both musical and familiar, rose in Peter's mind. *"He is yours to command until the moon grows full. Make haste! Make haste!"*

SUNLIGHT REFLECTED OFF METAL HELMETS, OFF CHARIOT wheels. Servants wearing only short white kilts sprinkled water on the racetrack to keep the dust from rising.

Quite close to the track, on a wooden platform constructed especially for this occasion, sat Nephia, straight and proud. In her lap she held Khaibit. She stroked him tenderly, knowing how crowds made him skittish, and whispered affectionate words into his ear.

Today, the princess wore a clean white linen shift with a wide jeweled collar. Her hair was pulled back from her head and woven into twice as many braids as usual. Festooned with lotus blossoms and surrounded by servants waving ostrich-plume fans, hers was clearly the place of honor.

On a slightly higher platform next to Nephia's sat the Pharaoh, wearing his heavy double crown. He smiled shakily at his daughter, wishing that he could escape this torment of chariot racing and return to his quiet chamber. Only for Nephia, his beloved child, would he endure this equestrian folly.

Nephia reached over to her father, taking his hand. Most likely, she confided, the first horse to cross the marker in front of the platform at the end of the race's seventh and final lap would be her own swift white favorite.

Behind the Pharaoh and his daughter, throngs of noble spectators sitting in row upon row of mud-brick bleachers craned their necks to see the Princess, while in the distance peasants stood in the hot sun, waiting.

Opposite, on the inside of the track, a more modest platform had been erected. Here stood Tachu, dressed in a long crimson gown. Framed by her ample wig, Tachu's face was expectant. Her eyes, lined in black, darted among the chariot drivers. Now Tachu brought the serpent scepter up, over her head. The crowd hushed. Down the road, the drivers calmed their horses. All eyes were on the Pharaoh's sister. With a nod toward Nephia, Tachu began to circle the golden staff in the air slowly, slowly, seven times. Then, with a savage thrust, Tachu flung the scepter to the ground. The race was begun!

7

WITH THE MUMMY'S VOICE REVERBERATING INside his head, Peter stood motionless on the sidewalk. One hand rested on the dog's sleek back. He didn't notice that the rain had stopped, that a bright August sun now beat down from a cloudless sky. He just stood there, flicking his chipped tooth with his tongue as the taxi disappeared around the corner of Twenty-seventh Street.

Mrs. Harring, meanwhile, inspected their new pet. "You know, I believe this dog is the same color as our couch. Not that we'll let him up on the furniture or anything, but it is nice that he matches."

Rodent checked the underside of the dog. "Boy time!" he announced.

Peter hadn't moved a muscle.

"Earth to Peter!" His mother waved her hand in front of his eyes. "You'll have to go to the deli and get him some food." She deposited a ten-dollar bill into his palm. "Bring me the change."

Peter looked blankly at the money.

"Let's go," Rodent said, becoming accustomed to steering his dazed friend about. "Man, you throw a penny into the pool and bingo! You get a dog! Me, I throw in a dime, I get zilch."

"Rode," Peter began as they crossed the street in front of the deli.

"Now what?"

"I . . . heard it again."

"Heard what?"

"The mummy. The Princess. She sent me the dog."

"Oh, sure. Right."

Peter cupped the dog's head in his hand and pressed him close. "You think I'm going crazy, Rode?"

"Sounds like it."

"Plus she said he is mine to command"—he looked down at the dog—"until the full moon."

"Come off it, Pete!"

"You think I could make this stuff up?"

"Why don't you just take care of man's best friend here while I get him some food." Rodent disappeared into the deli and reappeared with a bag of kibbles and two cans of Vita Pup. Then they headed back up the block to Peter's apartment building, the dog at his master's side.

"Thanks, Linton," Rodent said to the uniformed doorman who let them in.

Linton eyed the dog. "Ears like a bat, I'd say. What kind is he?"

"Don't know," said Rodent. "We found him in a taxi just now, during the storm."

"Storm?" Linton frowned. "What storm?"

"Half an hour ago. It was raining buckets."

"Not here it wasn't. Wish it would, though. Might break this heat."

Waiting for the elevator, Peter felt his damp T-shirt sticking to his skin and wondered how it was possible that there'd be a raging storm on Eighty-second Street and blue skies fifty blocks south.

"So what are you going to call him, Pete?" asked Rodent. "Let's see . . . you found him in a storm. How about Sprinkles? Or Puddles?"

His friend didn't seem to be listening.

"No," Rodent answered himself. "That makes it sound like he's not housebroken."

That got a faint smile out of Peter, but he shook his head. "He needs a dignified name."

In the elevator, Rodent punched 19. "Dignified, dignified . . ." He wouldn't have said anything to hurt Peter's feelings, but he thought maybe a name with some spunk was more the ticket. This dog needed pepping up. "How about Sir Archibald Pooper-Scooper the Third?"

As Rodent babbled, the dog stared up at Peter with his soulful eyes. Those eyes—they seemed to draw Peter in, to fill his mind with a chorus of distant voices. And as he listened, one word emerged. In an almost dreamy way, Peter repeated what he had heard: "Pharaoh."

"Pharaoh?" said Rodent. "Pete, haven't you had enough Egyptian stuff for one day? Can't you call him Benji or Fido or something?"

Peter shrugged. "That's his name."

———

When the elevator doors parted on the nineteenth floor, Peter's sister, Erin, was standing right outside, waiting for them. As usual, she had on a bright blue baseball cap with her carrot-colored ponytail sticking out above the adjustable band in the back. Green letters stitched on the front of the cap spelled out ROCKET SCIENTIST.

"Guess what?" she said in her gruff little voice. "We went on a field trip to the waterworks today and, boy, is the water you drink ever dis*gusting* before they put it through the filters, and Mrs. Bailey told us that they never really get all the yucky stuff out. I can't believe Mom let us get a dog."

"Not *us*, Erin," said Peter. "Me. This is *my* dog."

"His snout's really long. You know what? The average dog has a sense of smell that's one hundred times more powerful than a human's."

"Gee, Erin," said Rodent, pretending to be puzzled, "does that mean this dog smells better than you do?"

"Yes, I just told you . . . Oh, I get it. Very funny, Rodent." Erin turned to her brother. "He's not a purebred, is he? With a purebred, you can count on the type of dog you're getting, but with a mutt, you just never know."

Peter wished that Pharaoh would growl at Miss Know-it-All for that comment, but he didn't. Come to think of it, the dog hadn't growled or whimpered or barked at all.

"He's got pretty eyes," Erin said, walking backward toward their door. "Mrs. Bailey has pretty eyes, too. Maybe we could name him Bailey."

"Forget it, Erin." Peter pushed past her and went inside. "No way am I naming my dog after your science teacher. Besides, he's already got a name. Pharaoh."

"We studied ancient Egyptians last year in third grade," said Erin, not missing a beat. "They used to shave their hair off because every one of them had head lice and they wore those wigs 'cause they were totally bald. And you know what else?"

Peter, Rodent, and Pharaoh managed to escape her "what else" by sprinting into Peter's room and shutting the door.

"And stay out!" Peter called. "We're changing!"

Peter pulled off his dirty khakis and put on dry jeans and a T-shirt. Even though Rodent was a head taller than Peter, he wasn't any bigger around, and so he fit into a pair of Peter's cutoffs.

With a towel he had dropped on his floor a few showers ago, Peter dried the dog. "That's my boy," he murmured. "Let's have another look at your tag."

As Peter held the disk that hung from Pharaoh's collar, he began to feel pins and needles in his scalp, the way he had right after he'd kissed the Princess. The metal was smooth to the touch, and so glossy it nearly glowed. "Hey, Rode, this is gold."

"Oh, sure, Pete. A solid-gold dog tag. Right."

Again, Peter ran his finger over the disk and looked intently at the design etched into the metal. He saw clearly now that it wasn't any baseball inside a football. It was an eye. Over it arched a brow and extending from its bottom were two lines, one straight and the other curving up at the end.

"Oh, my gosh! Rode, come here, look at this. It's the eye!"

Rodent frowned. "Okay, maybe it is an eye. So what?"

"Rodent! Dog collars don't have *eyes* on them! And it's like that eye of what's-his-name on the mummies' coffins. See? I told you the mummy sent me the dog. Here's proof. What more do you need?"

"Lots." Rodent picked up Peter's hairbrush from the dresser. "We have to get your mind off mummies." He began brushing the dog and telling a complicated story about going street-combing the night before with Lucinda, hunting for sculpture materials, and meeting this guy who helped them carry an abandoned La-Z-Boy recliner up to their apartment and who claimed to have pitched for the Yankees in the seventies and swore he could get them free seats for a game, right on the third-base line.

Peter tried to listen, tried to forget all about hearing voices, until Erin's voice projected loud and clear through the door. "That dog'll have to have shots, you know, so he won't get rabies and start foaming at the mouth and biting people. And you know what? If you get bitten by a rabid dog, you have to get *seven* shots, and they stick the needle right into your stomach!"

Peter threw open the door but Erin was saved from serious bodily harm by their mother, who waltzed into his bedroom with a silky green dress on a hanger and her new beaded evening bag. "Aren't they perfect together?"

"You'll knock 'em dead, Mom."

"Listen, I've got a chicken in the oven and I'm making potato salad. You can stay and eat with us, can't you, Rode?"

"Oh, thanks, Mrs. H. I'll call and find out."

A genuine mom-roasted chicken would be a welcome departure from the Chinese food which he and Lucinda dined on night after night. Their apartment was directly over Szechuan Balcony Restaurant, and in return for not working with her power tools during dining hours, the restaurant's owner gave Lucinda a most attractive discount on takeout. They'd tried every single item on the Szechuan Balcony menu at least once, including Crispy Sea Bass Hunan Style, a whole fish that came with its head still on and a pair of dead white eyes staring out. And besides, Rodent knew that Lucinda was in the middle of creating another one of her Lady Liberty sculptures and would be just as happy to nibble solo on leftovers from one of the dozens of white cardboard cartons stacked in their refrigerator.

"We'll eat about seven," said Mrs. Harring. "Byron should be home from the agency by then."

"Hey, Rodent," said Erin, inching into Peter's room as Mrs. Harring exited, "did I show you my new skeleton? It's a squirrel. It used to be in the science room at school, but it freaked some first-grader out and he started screaming and his mother called the school and complained, so Mrs. Bailey said I could have it."

"No, Erin, Rodent does not want to see your sickening squirrel skeleton. He wants to help me feed Pharaoh."

"Come on, big fella." Rodent helped Peter coax the dog in the direction of the kitchen. "Din-din!"

But Pharaoh barely sniffed at the brown blob of food that Peter scraped into a cereal bowl. His expression made it clear that it was no-go with the Vita Pup.

"Maybe he's sick," suggested Erin. "Maybe you picked up a really contagiously sick dog."

Pharaoh gave Erin a sniff similar to the one he'd just given the lump of Vita Pup and then walked in a dignified manner into the entry hall just as the phone started to ring.

"Grab it, will you, Erin?" Mrs. Harring called. "And would you boys wash and slice the tomatoes, please?"

Rodent had gotten the tomatoes out of the crisper and Peter was testing the knife blade like a skilled surgeon when Erin called, "Mom! It's somebody named Western Union." Then, seconds later, he fumbled the knife and nearly nicked a knuckle as he heard his mother cry, *"What?"*

Peter ran into the living room, with Rodent at his heels. Erin had beat them both.

"Would you please read that again for me?" Mrs. Harring was sitting straight up on the couch with Pharaoh curled on the floor beside her. "I'm afraid I didn't get it all the first time."

"What's wrong?" whispered Peter.

His mother shushed him away as she groped for a pencil among the jumble on the coffee table and began to scribble furiously on a scrap of paper. "You're sure you've got the right Harring?" she said at last. "Byron Kingsley Harring? Well, thank you very much." She hung up and sank back on the couch, stunned.

"What, what, what?" Erin demanded.

"It's very odd," Mrs. Harring began. "That was a

telegram from a lawyer who is handling the estate of a great-aunt of your father's, someone I've never even heard him mention—a Kathryn Coffin.''

"Her name's Coffin?'' asked Peter.

"Like where you put dead people?'' asked Erin.

"Did she leave you a million dollars?'' asked Rodent.

"Not in cash, Rode, but evidently she's left us a town-house down on Third Street.''

Peter's hands felt clammy. There was something about this phone call that bothered him. "I didn't know Dad was related to anyone named Coffin,'' he said.

"It's probably all a big mistake,'' said his mother. "But wouldn't it be nice if it isn't?'' She got up from the couch. "Now, not a word about this until your father's had a chance to catch his breath.'' Mrs. Harring drifted toward the kitchen. "Imagine, a whole town-house just for us.''

THE DRUMMING GREW LOUDER AS THE HORSES GALLOPED UP
the track toward Nephia, approaching the viewing
stands in a struggling pack.

As the horses flew around the curve, their hooves
digging at the dirt, Khaibit lept from Nephia's lap to
the platform. He turned and rubbed his head against
her leg, as if trying to get Nephia away from this pound-
ing noise, this dusty air. Again and again, he pressed
against his girl.

Nephia reached down and gave the cat a quick pat.
Then she straightened and clapped with excitement
as her favorite took the lead. Her father mopped his
brow. Past the starting point the white horse ran.
Nephia's platform was so close to the track that she
could feel her heart throbbing with the hoofbeats each
time the horses galloped by.

On the fourth lap, three horses pulled ahead of the
rest, the white horse among them. Around again, the

chargers sped. The three kept the lead: a cream color, a midnight black, and the white. Nephia called out to encourage him. Even as she cheered, a driver in a golden helmet lashed a roan steed ahead on the inside of the track. Faster and faster he urged the horse, his chariot tilting dangerously, one wheel off the ground.

Across the track, Tachu's eyes were wide, eager. Her fists clutched at her dress.

Khaibit sensed danger. He nipped at Nephia's ankle. He must get her away from this confusion. The Princess merely shook her foot. Khaibit meowed a desperate warning, but his yowling was lost in the deafening noise.

Now the gold-helmeted driver drew alongside the lead chariots. Recklessly, he beat his horse, demanding more speed, more! His horse's eyes were wild, its mouth foaming as it fought its way ahead. And then, almost invisibly, the driver tugged the reins to the right, toward the stands. The wheels of the chariot sliced into the crowd! The wooden stands swayed from the impact and cracked. The royal fan bearers screamed. In confusion, they tried to flee. Still the driver beat the panicked animal, and it plunged ahead, straight toward the Pharaoh.

Paralyzed with fear, Amenhut felt his heart stop beating as the frantic beast charged on.

In a split second, Nephia leaped over to her father's platform. She lunged toward the horse, grabbing its neck. Caught off-guard by Nephia's jump, the horse veered from its path. It whinnied and reared. Nephia clutched the horse's mane and was lifted up. She tried to keep her grip, to throw her leg over its back, but the horse kicked its hooves wildly in the air. Nephia felt her grasp slipping. *Crack!* Again, the driver lashed the horse. Fury-eyed, it bucked, hurtling Nephia to the ground. *Crack!* The terrified horse trampled the Princess under its heavy hooves, vaulted out of the crowd, and raced away down the track.

Too late, movement returned to the Pharaoh's limbs. He rushed to his daughter, gathering her in his arms.

Across the track, Tachu whispered unknown syllables as she stared in horror at her brother cradling his only child. Those who observed her at this moment believed her to be too stricken with grief over the terrible accident to rush to Nephia's side.

From beneath the platform where his girl had sat so straight and proud just moments before, the Spirit-cat looked on.

8

THE BOYS MADE A BED FOR PHARAOH IN PETER'S room, out of a beat-up quilt and some pillows. Then Rodent knotted a length of twine onto the dog's collar as a makeshift leash, and he and Peter took Pharaoh out for a walk. Dodging hordes of pedestrians eager to get home on a Friday evening, they reached Animal World just before closing time, and Peter bought Pharaoh a sturdy black leather leash.

As they headed over to the park, Rodent tried to understand Peter's mood. "Some rich old lady leaves you a mansion and you're sulking about it?"

"I don't know, something seems weird." Peter shrugged. "Her name, for instance." He didn't even want to say it.

"She should have left it to me," said Rodent. "I wouldn't care if her name was Draculina la Corpse."

On the walk, Pharaoh didn't seem one bit interested in what Rodent called "reading the doggie newspaper"—sniffing fire hydrants and car tires and trash baskets for scent messages left by other canines. He didn't raise his leg next to a single spindly city tree or leave a deposit next to the curb for Peter to scoop up with the pages of *The New York Times* which he had brought along for that purpose. Past poodles and shepherds and Scotties and wrinkly sharpeis and mutts of every hue and size—all sniffing and yapping and straining at their leashes to get to one another—Pharaoh walked calmly at his master's side. The other dogs took no notice of him.

After a second dry run around the park, they started for home.

Walking back, Peter noticed that the moon, slender as a single parenthesis, had risen. It was a new moon now, but new moons grew. And then what?

"Rode?" he said. "When's the full moon?"

"Funny you should ask," said Rodent as they passed a storefront window where Madam Diana, Palmist, had hung her calendar. On the bottom right-hand corner of the day's date, Friday, August 17, was a slim curved line and tiny letters spelling out *New Moon*. Peter traced his finger along the glass until he came to the square for Friday, August 31. Here, the slim line had expanded into a circle. *Full Moon*.

On the other side of the window, a woman with glossy black hair beckoned.

"Hey, that's it, Pete! Get your fortune told! For only two-fifty, Madam Diana can tell you why the mummy sent you the pooch here, and what you're supposed to do about it!"

"Forget it, Rode." Peter walked rapidly up the block away from the palmist's window.

Rodent caught up with him at the corner. "Lucinda got her palm read once," he confessed. "The Madam said she was going to meet a tall, dark stranger who would change her life, but it never happened. She'd probably just tell you the same thing."

Peter never guessed that, had Madam Diana read the lines of his palm, she most certainly would have delivered this very same message.

"Dad's home!" Erin called to the boys, who had retreated once again to Peter's room.

Rodent rubbed the dog's back with both hands. "Come on, Pharaoh baby. Time to make a good impression on Papa."

Limply, Peter trailed Rodent into the living room, where his friend immediately started selling his dog to his father.

"So what do you think of Pharaoh, Mr. H.? A magnificent specimen, isn't he?" Rodent coaxed the dog over to Mr. Harring, who was just easing into his favorite chair, loosening his tie.

"Very amusing, Rode," said Mr. Harring. "Now will you kindly remove this beast from our apartment before we all get fleas?"

"No joke, Mr. H."

Peter hurried to Pharaoh's side. "Mom said I could keep him."

"Why, of all the harebrained ideas! Jean, what on earth . . ."

"Byron, just relax while I fix you something cold to drink."

Byron Harring ran a hand through his thick mane of red hair. Then he closed his eyes and nodded his approval of this suggestion. He'd been an advertising executive with the Goodchild Agency for twenty years, and was, as he was fond of saying, the brains of the operation, in charge of coming up with brilliant campaigns for every product imaginable. His most famous was the Ajax Aspirin ad, where two little pills with arms and legs danced around inside a person's stomach.

Mr. Harring took a long sip of the drink his wife handed him, before he peered down at the dog still sitting at attention in front of his chair. Just for a second, the dog's yellow eyes locked with his brown ones. Then Pharaoh blinked and lightly placed a paw on his knee. "What do you know, he shakes hands." Mr. Harring took the paw and pumped it up and down. "Fine, boy! Yes! You're congratulating me, aren't you?" He chuckled, letting go of Pharaoh's paw. "In fact, you may all congratulate me."

"Congratulations," said Rodent.

"For what?" said Erin.

"Oh, just for landing a new account for the agency, that's all. Just a big, fat, megabucks account."

"That's wonderful, Byron," said Mrs. Harring.

"Here before you sits the person who will help American consumers understand that they can't live without Naper Toilet Paper, which is soft yet sturdy, tears straight across every time, and, square for square, is extremely economical compared to other brands." He took another sip of his drink. "This is going to be big. Very big."

"You'll have to tell us all about it while we eat," said Mrs. Harring. "Come on, everyone, to the table."

During dinner, Peter seemed lost in his own thoughts, but both Erin and Rodent fidgeted like crazy as Mr. Harring explained idea after idea for his toilet-paper campaign. Only the sternest glances from Mrs. Harring kept them from blurting out the news about the Coffin house. Mr. Harring went on so long that Rodent had to go home before Mrs. Harring broached the subject.

"Well, Byron, we've had some interesting news, too. Does the name Kathryn Coffin mean anything to you?"

"Kathryn Coffin," mused Mr. Harring. "Didn't I work with her on the Chunky Cheese Spread account?"

"Oh, dear," said Peter's mother. "We're the wrong Harrings." And then she explained.

"Maybe she is some distant relative," Mr. Harring said when she finished, "but I've never heard of her. We'll just have to wait until we get some more details. Coffin, eh?"

Peter wished people would stop saying that name.

Late that night, he woke suddenly from a strange and vivid dream that seemed on the brink of revealing something of tremendous importance. But what? He lay there, feeling more exhausted than ever. Yet, try as he might, he couldn't remember the dream.

He stared out his window at the spire of the Empire State Building, illuminated now in blue and orange to honor the first-place Mets, and his mind drifted away to Princess Nephia. What had she called him? *A man of the future.* Well, she had lived three thousand years ago, so this certainly was the future. A man? Someday, he supposed he would be, if that growth spurt ever got going. Peter tried to recall the rest of her words: *Bring back the treasure of my soul.* What sorts of things did souls treasure? Was it something carried by the army of servants painted on the sides of her coffin? And if so, just where was he supposed to find it? He'd have to wait, he guessed, until she chose to tell him more about it. Or until something happened to make it clear. Something with Pharaoh, maybe. *He is yours to command until the moon grows full.* But just what was he supposed to command the dog to do? And what would happen after the full moon? It seemed that all he had were questions, without a single solitary answer.

When the phone rang on Saturday morning, Peter picked it up.

"My deepest sympathy and condolences on the passing of your relation," a raspy voice said into his ear. "I am the executor of Kathryn Coffin's will, Jarvis Scrull."

"Jarvis *Skull*?"

"Close enough," the lawyer cackled. "Close enough. Do I have the pleasure of speaking with Mr. Harring?"

"You want my dad," Peter managed. "I'll get him."

Mr. Harring spoke to the lawyer for a long time, jotting down notes all the while. Peter hovered nervously nearby, fending off Erin's persistent question of "What skull?"

After what seemed an eternity, Mr. Harring hung up. "Jean!" he called. "Jean!"

Mrs. Harring hurried into the living room.

"Kathryn Coffin was, in fact, my mother's grandmother's sister," he announced.

"Oh, Byron!" said Peter's mother. "You mean we're the right Harrings after all?"

"The closest living relatives. That lawyer says we've inherited a six-story townhouse, complete with furnishings. It's ours, free and clear!"

"Six stories!" Mrs. Harring exclaimed.

"According to Scrull, Kathryn Coffin was one of seven children who grew up in the house. In time, her mother died, and all her brothers and sisters married and moved away, but Kathryn stayed to keep house for her father, who was some sort of scientist."

"Oh, cool!" said Erin.

"After Professor Coffin's death, nearly thirty years ago, Kathryn retired from the outside world and never left the house again."

"What'd she do," asked Erin, "send out for pizza every night?"

"Evidently, the daughter of an old family servant stayed to help her. So it's no wonder we never heard of her."

"How many bedrooms, Byron?"

Mr. Harring squinted to decipher his notes. "Four bedrooms, a library, some kind of a laboratory . . ."

"For my experiments!" shouted Erin.

"We'll see." Mr. Harring read from his pad of paper again. "It has a full basement, an attic, and a big garden out back."

"Pinch me, Byron! I must be dreaming!"

"You'll believe it next Wednesday, my dear." Mr.

Harring hugged his wife and began twirling her around the living room. "That's when Jarvis Scrull is sending over the key to the Coffin house!"

"Hold it!" Peter looked from his father to his mother. "Don't you think something a little weird is going on when you inherit a *Coffin* house and get keys from a Mr. *Skull*?"

"Scrull, Peter . . ."

"But don't you at least think it's a little *unusual*?"

"No," said Mrs. Harring. "I think it's just perfect."

"Well, there is one rather unusual stipulation in Kathryn Coffin's will," began Mr. Harring.

"I told you," said Peter.

"Shhh. What's that, Byron?"

"It says we have to move into the house within the month or it will go to the next closest living relative." Mr. Harring scratched his head. "I suppose that would be my cousin Rufus in Cincinnati."

Mrs. Harring folded her arms across her chest. "We might as well start packing right now, then," she said, "because there is no way we are letting a six-story Manhattan townhouse slip through our fingers and go to Cousin Rufus!"

NEPHIA LAY ON HER GOLDEN BED. SHE SEEMED TO SLEEP peacefully, her small hands clasped on her chest, her cat curled at her shoulder. The women in gray weeping by the bedside were the only sign that Nephia would never awaken.

Now the Pharaoh, bent with grief, entered her chamber. Behind him came Tachu. She advanced boldly to the bed, waving the mourners away. With a sweep of her hand, she tried to shoo Khaibit off the bed, but the cat did not stir. Hastily, Tachu withdrew her hand and turned to the Pharaoh. The cat, too, was dead!

Slowly, Amenhut advanced. He reached out and caressed the head of his lovely girl. Then, with a tender touch, he stroked her cat.

Amenhut understood. Loyal Khaibit, imbued with the spirit of Nephia's mother, his beloved Hapii, had died of a broken heart. How well the Pharaoh understood, for his heart, too, was breaking.

Beckoning to a servant, the Pharaoh proclaimed that Khaibit's devotion would be honored for eternity. He gave instructions for the Spirit-cat to be mummified and entombed along with his beautiful child.

For the first time since Nephia had been struck by the horse's hooves, Amenhut felt a small degree of comfort as he thought of the Spirit-cat joining the seven spirits of Nephia. Now they would be together forever in the Land of the Dead, just as they had been in this Land of the Living.

9

"COFFIN, SCHMOFFIN," PETER MUTTERED AS HE clipped the leash to Pharaoh's collar. "Skull, Scrull. I don't like this."

Over their customary Saturday morning pancakes, the Harrings had decided to walk down to Third Street to inspect their new property.

"Even if we can't get inside yet," Mrs. Harring had said, "at least we can nose around."

Mr. Harring set a rapid pace down Third Avenue. He had things to do on the TP account, and he wanted to get back to them as soon as possible. "I was thinking we should concentrate on softness as a virtue," he explained as they walked. "Picture this skier, ready to head down a slope, and all of a sudden rolls of toilet paper start falling from the sky, and the guy just stands there, letting them bounce off his head, like he doesn't even feel them. Then a voice-over says, 'Naper Toilet Paper . . . it's soft as snow.' " He paused. "Well? Jean?"

"I'm not sure about the association with snow."

"No?"

"It's just that snow is so cold . . ."

Peter and Erin fell behind their parents as they walked past vendors at tables selling scarves, socks, and "Books for a Buck"; past an aromatic shish-kebab cart, which interested Pharaoh not at all; past a man in a white doctor's coat offering free foot exams, which interested Erin immensely.

"I want to find out if I have hammertoes," she said, scanning the leaflet the white-coated man had handed her.

"Some other time," said Peter, nodding to indicate their parents waiting for them on the next corner. Reluctantly, Erin handed the pamphlet back and walked with her brother and his dog down to Third Street.

In the middle of the block, dozens of serious-looking motorcycles were parked along the curb outside a townhouse. A painting of a large skull with a wing jutting out of its brain cavity hung over the front door, along with a sign proclaiming: HELL'S ANGELS HEADQUARTERS.

Mr. Harring read aloud the numbers of the houses on the south side of the block. "There it is!" he exclaimed. "Our home, sweet home!"

"Oh, cool!" said Erin. "We're moving across the street from a biker gang!"

Mr. Harring chuckled. "You know, I've always harbored a secret desire to take a Harley out for a spin."

"Well, dear," said his wife, "if we get to know our new neighbors, you may get your chance."

Outside the Angels' house, a trio of middle-aged, pot-

bellied men with long, shaggy hair and faded blue tat-
toos running the length of their arms leaned against
their motorcycles, talking with a frizzy-haired woman
in a metal-studded leather vest.

"You know what?" said Erin."To get a tattoo, somebody sticks a needle into your skin and then puts dye
in the hole and if they're not careful it can poison your
blood."

"I appreciate the warning," said Peter, almost thankful for Erin's incessant babbling. At least, for a while,
it had taken his mind off the Coffin house.

It might have been a cheerful house once, but now
its red bricks were dark with city grime. Ivy, thick and
large-leaved, covered the sides and had begun to invade
the front as well. A door with peeling paint was set at
street level, beneath stone steps which led up to a once-
grand front door on the second floor. Projecting from
the fourth story was a bay window, and the roof
spouted four chimneys. Encircling the house was a
spiked wrought-iron fence. Peter tightened his grip on
Pharaoh's leash. Unlikely as it seemed, some sixth sense
told him that this ruin held a mummy's treasure.

"I bet it's full of dust and bats and spiderwebs and
giant sewer rats," Erin said.

"Oh, honey, it's just old, that's all," said Mrs. Harring.
She lifted the latch on the gate and the others followed
her up the steps. Peter tried to peer into a window, but
all the shades were pulled down tight.

Next, his mother led the way along a narrow alley
by the side of the house that opened up on a large,
overgrown garden. High, vine-covered walls enclosed

a yard with a pair of lofty trees growing at the rear. The leaves of the trees spread in a broad canopy over the yard, obscuring any view of the sky.

"Oh, Byron!" exclaimed Mrs. Harring. "From the street, no one would ever guess there's such a fine back yard. Why, these brambles are actually rosebushes! This must have been a lovely garden once."

The family meandered around the grounds, making minor discoveries—a crumbling birdbath, a pair of rustic chairs on a back porch that stretched the width of the house, a patch of poison ivy, and, just before the alleyway, a pair of wooden cellar doors set at an angle into the foundation.

"These aren't locked," called Mr. Harring as he pulled one door open. "I'll go down and see if there's a way into the house."

A dank odor wafted up from the cellar and Peter felt a chill pass through him. It wasn't just the spooky old house that made the gooseflesh rise. No, something wasn't right down there. He could sense it, and he thought Pharaoh could, too, from the way he was crouched, as if ready to spring.

Mr. Harring tramped down the stairs. At the bottom, he yanked a string, turning on a bare light bulb. "It's cool down here," his voice echoed up. "And storage space galore!" His footsteps sounded on the cellar floor, growing fainter and finally disappearing altogether.

After what seemed to Peter a long time, Mr. Harring clicked off the light and jogged back up to the yard. "What a wine cellar we're going to have!" he exclaimed, shutting the doors. "But there's no entrance to the house from down there, so we'll just have to wait to see it on Wednesday, when Scrull sends over the key." He consulted his watch. "Let's get going now. I've got to rethink that toilet paper."

As Peter retraced his steps to the street, he noticed that the top floor of the old house had two south-facing dormer windows which stuck out from the roof like a pair of gawking eyes. Could his parents really think this eerie old house was charming? He shuddered and Pharaoh nuzzled his arm. Always before, contact with the dog had soothed him, but now, for the first time, it merely increased his dread.

ONE AFTER ANOTHER, THE YEARS FOLLOWING NEPHIA'S funeral passed, until more than twenty had gone by.

For Amenhut, these were lonely, painful years. He left the rule of his kingdom to his vizier, a fair and honest man, and kept to himself as much as possible. Although he knew that the gods did not wish him to grieve, he could not help missing those who had traveled before him to the Land of the Dead. The only thing that lightened the load of his sorrow was composing poems about his loved ones.

For Tachu, these were bitter, angry years. She delved into her midnight sorcery with increased passion and during the day took advantage of Amenhut's absence to ingratiate herself with the kingdom's Chief Priest. From him, Tachu hoped to wheedle a look at the Forbidden Scroll.

For Nephia's *sahu*, these first years of the afterlife were spent traveling to meet Osiris, lord of the underworld. Since Khaibit's mummy shared her own mummy's coffin, the spirit of the little cat was at her side as she undertook this most perilous journey, by boat, passing through countless gateways guarded by evil animal-headed gods. Only by reciting spells from the Book of the Dead did Nephia finally arrive at the Hall of Two Truths. There, Osiris and forty-two judges waited. They looked on as Anubis, a god with a human body and the head of a jackal, took Nephia's heart and put it on one side of a scale. On the other side, he put Maat's Feather of Truth. Because Nephia's heart was pure, it was lighter than the feather, so Nephia was given leave to approach the throne of Osiris and then travel to her new life in the Fields of Peace, which were remarkably similar to the Land of Egypt. Wherever she wandered in the Land of the Dead, Khaibit was at her side.

For Nephia's mummified remains left in the burial chamber, the years were dark and silent except for the faint footsteps of the Tomb Guards and the skittering of small creatures across the floor.

And then one night a sharp blow to the seal of her chamber shattered the stillness. Torchlight flickered and three men peered in through the door. The first stepped over the threshold. Stout as a stuffed goose, he held a smoky torch in one hand and with his other arm, ending in a handless stump, he beckoned his companions into Nephia's sanctuary. In crept a smooth-cheeked boy, bare but for a ragged waistcloth. After him came the third, tall and lean, with a jagged white scar running down his face from the bridge of his nose to his chin.

With no care for the dead, the robbers grasped what

they could sell to the living. The stout one propped his torch in a holder on the wall and struggled to open a sack. Into it, the boy threw Nephia's earthly treasures: a jewelry box, a small harp, a tambourine, a little gold doll's cup, a wooden crocodile with a hinged jaw that opened and closed. In went Nephia's favorite necklaces, bracelets, anklets, rings. Amenhut's scrolls rested on the floor of the tomb, but these the robbers kicked aside.

The fat one whispered gruffly to his taller companion. They must not forget the words of the one who had arranged this little visit, she of the staring eyes: all the riches that they could carry from the tomb they might keep. But to her they must deliver the cat mummy from inside the coffin. It and it alone she desired.

The tall thief and the boy pushed up the lid of the great stone sarcophagus and, straining with effort, lowered it to the tomb floor. Then they removed the cover from the first case, the second, the third, at last exposing the mummies of Nephia and her cat. The boy grabbed Khaibit and threw him into the bag as the tall thief's coarse hands rifled Nephia's linen wrappings, ripping them, tangling them in his thoughtless search for scarabs. When they had found every last gem, they flung the mummy back into its case. As soon as they had emptied the tomb, they would put a torch to that mummy. How it would blaze! And then the seven spirits of the Princess could not come back to this world to take their vengeance on those who had violated her tomb.

But before they could complete their plans, the robbers were startled by a sudden sound. The Tomb Guards! The tall one snatched the sack, the fat one stubbed out the torch on the floor, and the three fled through the tomb door into a narrow passageway where no guards would find them.

Nephia's tomb was empty now of thieves, and of most of her treasures as well. The sound of running feet grew fainter. The dusty air swirled in the fading light. Then, with a flapping of wings and a quiver of shadows, a swarm of bats swooped in. So many! Their ripe, earthy scent filled the tomb. They darted in all directions and then, one by one, found purchase on the ceiling of the tomb. Folding their wings around their bodies, they clung upside down, waiting above Nephia's head for sleep to claim them.

10

ON WEDNESDAY AFTERNOON, RODENT WAS
again leaning against the lobby wall in Peter's
apartment building. At last Peter emerged from the elevator, his football under one arm, his dog at his side.

"It's Harring the Daring and Mighty Dog!" Rodent
rubbed Pharaoh vigorously, but didn't get a rise out of
him. Some dull mutt, he thought as he straightened up.
"So, tonight's the night, huh? Going to check out the
Coffin house? Can I come?"

"You better, 'cause there's some connection between
this house and the mummy, and maybe you can help
me figure out what it is. There's only a week and a half
left till the full moon."

"Aw, Pete, you're losing touch with reality."

"*I'm* losing touch? My mom's told some NYU professor he can sublet our apartment and she's got a moving van coming on Saturday and we're supposed to
pack up and go live in a house we've never even been
in, and you think *I'm* losing touch?"

They walked a few blocks in silence, west on Twenty-eighth Street. As they waited for a traffic light to change, a policeman mounted on a tall chestnut horse clopped slowly up Madison Avenue. Pharaoh pressed against Peter's leg.

"Hey, he's shaking." Peter reached down to soothe the dog, but he kept shivering until the horse and rider were out of sight. "It's okay, boy. It was just some old horse."

At the entrance to Madison Square Park, Peter hesitated. "Hold it. You think Howie's around?"

"Nah. Charlie told me that, since soccer's over, he mostly skateboards up in Central Park with his junior-high buddies." Rodent kicked at some crumpled newspaper in the middle of the sidewalk. "Come on, let's go over to the doggie section."

Dog walkers hung out together in the middle of the park, letting their dogs run free beneath the sign that commanded: KEEP YOUR DOG ON A LEASH. Now, with Pharaoh in tow, the boys headed toward the grassy area. On this hot, sticky weekday afternoon, they had the spot almost to themselves, except for a woman with a yellow Labrador and an eager little dachshund. Just as before, the other dogs took no notice of Pharaoh, and Pharaoh ignored them. The Lab and the dachshund both had their tongues out, panting in the August heat. Pharaoh wasn't panting; in fact, he seemed oddly cool. When Rodent tried to interest him in chasing a stick, he turned away, almost as if embarrassed, and sat down, so Peter coaxed him to a shady spot and looped his leash over the picket of a low fence enclosing a thornbush. "Stay here, boy, while Rodent and I toss the football."

Rodent threw first. Peter caught the ball, adjusted his fingers on the lacing, and called, "Here comes the bomb!"

Rodent stretched for the catch but missed. "Boy, for a short guy, you sure can throw. You could beat Howie for distance."

"That's all I need." Peter caught Rodent's throw on the bounce. "Then maybe he'd give me a bloody nose *and* a black eye."

They stepped closer and threw the football easily back and forth. But twice Peter caught the ball and held it, forgetting to throw it back.

"Hey, space case!" Rodent shouted after a faked pass provoked no reaction. "We don't have to toss the pigskin, you know."

"Guess I'm a little freaked out about . . . things."

The boys went back to where Pharaoh was resting, and sat down in the grass. Stroking the dog, Peter immediately felt his anxiety drain away. Pharaoh was the best thing that had ever happened to him. Dog walking was a great excuse for escaping the apartment and his mother's endless packing instructions, and Pharaoh made it even easier by never making a mess for him to scoop up. He'd never heard the dog bark or whine or growl and, as far as he could tell, he'd never eaten a single bite of his doggy chow or lapped water from his dish. And then there was the golden collar . . . In his head Peter knew that Pharaoh was far from ordinary, but in his heart he forgave these oddities and simply loved his dog. Now he unclipped Pharaoh's leash from his collar, tracing the outline of the eye on the tag with his finger.

"Hey, hey, what's this?" Rodent reached cautiously into the base of the sticker bush and pulled out a dirty but otherwise undamaged blue Frisbee. "Get ready, man's best friend." He sailed the disk up, not far from the dog, but Pharaoh simply sat. Rodent ran to get the Frisbee, brought it back, and held it in front Pharaoh's nose. "Get the scent. Now, fetch!"

Again he threw the Frisbee. And again Pharaoh stayed put. This time, when Rodent went to fetch it, he dropped to all fours on the ground, stuck the Frisbee in between his teeth, and began crawling back toward Pharaoh, demonstrating the proper technique. But when Rodent tossed the Frisbee again, Pharaoh didn't budge.

Rodent slammed the Frisbee to the ground. "What a dud dog!"

"Aw, he's just never done it before." Peter hugged Pharaoh and then picked up the Frisbee. "See, you're supposed to catch it in the air." The dog's solemn eyes traveled from Peter to the disk. "Come on, boy! Catch it for me!" As Peter launched the Frisbee up at a sharp angle, the dog exploded from his crouch. With a flying leap, he caught the disk a good five feet above the ground.

"All right!" shouted Peter. "Did you see that catch?"

Rodent squinted suspiciously at Pharaoh. "Let me try it."

Peter gave his friend the Frisbee and Rodent hurled it up. "Go get it, puppy!"

But the dog merely sat attentively on the grass.

Peter ran to pick up the Frisbee. "Here it goes, Pharaoh!"

Once more the dog sprang to life with an amazing midair catch.

Without exchanging a word, Peter and Rodent began taking turns throwing the Frisbee. Every time Rodent threw it, Pharaoh sat and watched. But each time his master threw it, Pharaoh bounded up and caught it.

At last Rodent flopped down under the tree again. "I take it all back. He's ready for the doggie Olympics!"

"He is mine to command, as the mummy said."

"Clearly," said Rodent, "a one-boy dog. Hey, there's a vendor down on Twenty-third Street. You hungry?"

"Always."

"Loan me enough for a dog—no offense intended, Mr. Pharaoh—and I'll go get the chow."

As they sat side by side in the shade, wolfing down their food, Rodent held out the end piece of his hot dog. "Here you go, Ruler of Egypt. Have some American haute cuisine." But Pharaoh didn't even sniff, so Rodent popped the bite into his own mouth, licking mustard from his fingers.

Peter got to his feet and clipped the leash to Pharaoh's collar. "I have to get home and do some packing."

Tossing the Frisbee back into the sticker bush, Rodent started up the path. "I'm ready for a . . . aw, rats! After that mummy's toe business, I should have known better than to trust Charlie Bemmelmann."

Peter swore never to trust Charlie again, and maybe not Rodent, either, for there, at the park entrance, stood Howie Krieger and a pair of his oversized buddies, grinning like sharks.

ON A STARLESS NIGHT, THREE WERE ADMITTED TO THE PHAR-
aoh's palace. One, with a scar running down his cheek,
concealed a parcel beneath his cloak. A stout man and
a boy followed him through long corridors to a chamber smelling of incense. There, they bowed low to a
woman in red sitting in an ebony chair.

This night, Tachu wore the cobra headdress over her
finest braided wig. The golden viper stared out at the
world through diamond eyes as cold and hard as the
pair of gorgeously painted brown eyes below it. These
eyes were failing now, but this was Tachu's secret. She
had many. For years, her skin had been massaged with
the finest unguents, keeping the lines of time at bay.
Only when she opened her mouth to speak to the
thieves did she reveal her true age, for long years of
chewing the bread of Egypt, which no amount of sifting
could render free of sand, had ground her teeth to
stubs.

Tachu stopped stroking the small green snake coiled at her wrist and motioned to the three. Come closer! She was ready to receive what they had stolen for her. Oh, so ready! She felt absolutely giddy with the perfection of her scheme. Not only did it violate the seven spirits of her wretched niece, spoiler of her chance to rule Egypt, but it would do something she hardly dreamed possible. How she blessed the day the High Priest, unbeknownst to the Pharaoh, had at last given in to her wiles and agreed, for a ridiculously high sum, to let her spend one evening with the Forbidden Scroll. And there she had found what she was looking for, written by no human hand: the list of ingredients for creating the Potion of Eternity.

Sting of Wasp and fang of Snake,
Sprout of root from young Mandrake,
Seven scales of Crocodile,
Seven droplets from the Nile,
Ibis feather, hair of Dog,
Tail of Lizard, eye of Frog,
Spleen of Eel and blood of Bat,
Knucklebone of Spirit-cat.

True, the Forbidden Scroll had listed the necessary items for the ancient enchantment, but it neglected to tell how to awaken their powers. Ah, but not for nothing was she a High Priestess at the altar of Set, god of darkness, and after the proper sacrifices—she knew the ones!—the evil god had granted her the knowledge to complete the ancient recipe and cast the simple but all-powerful spell.

> Grind into a powder fine,
> Sift it slowly, nine times nine.
> Boil at midnight, moonless sky,
> Who drinks of this shall never die.

Once she had the mummy of Khaibit in her hands, once she had unwrapped it and obtained just one tiny knucklebone of the Spirit-cat, then nothing could stop her. What did it matter now if her heart was heavy with sin? Or that she was unfit to journey to the Land of the Dead? She was never going to die, not once she drank the Potion!

The tall thief held out the small bundle. Tachu rose from her chair and stretched out her arms to receive it. He placed it in her hands. At last!

Tachu took no notice of the thieves bowing once more and backing out of her chamber. She did not hear their quick footsteps fade away down the palace hallways. She saw, heard, felt, smelled only the Spirit-cat.

Carrying the mummy over to a table, Tachu plucked at the linen bandages that time had stuck fast together. There. She found a loose piece, and after the first layer . . . but what was this? Tachu squinted down at the linen. Did her dimming eyes deceive her? What was this mark? It was not the linen stamp of Amenhut! Her brow creased in anger. This could not be Khaibit's mummy; it was no rare Spirit-cat! Those thieves! They had tricked her! With a violent swing of her arms, Tachu smashed the false cat to the floor.

Oooooh! Tachu's face convulsed with fury! Her heart hammered with rage. She would find those thieves, oh yes! They would be missing more than their hands when she was finished with them. She clenched her fists and shook them at fate, careless of the small green viper at her wrist. In her frenzy, Tachu never felt the prick of the serpent's tooth as it pierced her palm.

But . . . why was it becoming so difficult to breathe? What was this pain stabbing at her chest? Tachu clutched the golden chain at her throat. From it hung a blue leather pouch containing eleven powdered ingredients for the potion. All of them save one. It soothed her to feel them there, to know she was close, so close. But this pain! So fierce! It took her breath. She was gasping, choking! Tachu grabbed at the back of the ebony chair as she tumbled to the floor. Dying? Oh no! Not now. Not yet. Not her. Not without that . . . one . . . little . . . bone!

11

HOWIE BLOCKED THE SIDEWALK, ONE IMPRES-
sive sneaker poised on the rear of his skateboard. He stood between two oafish creeps that Peter
recognized as having spent several years in sixth grade
at P.S. 40 before moving on to junior high. One of them
toted a baseball bat over his shoulder, but Peter saw no
sign of a ball.

"Hey, you guys ever met the king of daredevils here?"
sneered Howie. "And his bean-pole pal, Ratboy?"

"That's, uh, Rodent."

"And now Harring's got another big rat following
him around." Howie pointed at Pharaoh.

"We were just leaving." Peter tried to squeeze past
Howie on the sidewalk. "Park's all yours."

"What's the hurry? I think there's something I have
to do first. Now, what was it? Oh, yeah!" Howie slapped
his hand to his flat forehead as if he'd just remembered.
"I gotta dare you!"

Peter's nose ached in anticipation.

"Pete!" Rodent cried. "The dog! Sic Pharaoh on him!"

Howie backed up a step.

Peter tightened his grip on Pharaoh's leash.

Rodent balled his hands into fists and punched the air. "Do it! Do it! Do it!" He started jumping up and down on the sidewalk. "Tell him, Pete! Tell him to go for Howie's throat!"

Howie took another step back, this time, perhaps, from Rodent.

Nephia's words rang inside Peter's head: *He is yours to command.* The dog stood at attention beside him, ready to obey.

"Come on, Pete!" Rodent turned to Howie. "This dog's gonna chew you up and spit you out!"

"Pharaoh!" commanded Peter. "Stay!"

The dog sat down on the sidewalk.

"Aw, Pete, no!" Rodent wailed. "No!"

Howie hesitated for a moment. Then he smiled and moved in on Peter."Okay, Harring the Daring! I dare that dog to sic me!"

"The dog doesn't take dares," said Peter flatly.

"Well, then, he's smarter than you are, dog-brain! I dare you to sock me in the nose!"

Peter sighed and stuck out his arm in the direction of Howie's breathing equipment. Half a second later, he was on the ground with bright drops of his own red blood splattering the pavement.

Howie held his palms up innocently. "Self-defense."

Then he and his sniggering sidekicks took turns stepping over Peter's prone body. Howie dropped his skateboard and pushed off down the path.

Peter took the hand Rodent offered and struggled to stand, mashing the hem of his T-shirt to his nose to slow the bleeding.

"Aw, Pete, you should have done it! Pharaoh could have taught him a lesson."

Over by the drinking fountain, the bully was now menacing a pair of little girls on roller skates. What a cretin, thought Peter. But what could he do?

With a click of his tongue, he summoned his dog and they left the park.

The boys were playing video games when Mrs. Harring came home from Bookworld that evening.

"Peter, I've got some news for . . . Oh, not again!"

Peter picked up the cold pack he'd gotten out of the freezer and held it to his swollen nose to hide it from his mother.

"It was that Howard, wasn't it?" Mrs. Harring dropped her briefcase with a thud. "I'm going to phone his mother and let her know that his violent behavior will not be tolerated."

"Don't, Ba. It'll just bake it worse."

Mrs. Harring sighed. "The only thing that will keep me from calling is if you'll *promise* to stay out of his way from now on."

"I prombis. You've got dews?" he asked, hoping to change the subject.

Peter's mother sat down across from the boys. "I finally got around to phoning the taxi dispatcher and no calls have come in about a missing dog, so I suppose he's yours."

Behind the cold pack, Peter grinned. He put his free

arm around Pharaoh's neck and pulled the dog closer, realizing that he'd never had the slightest doubt that Pharaoh belonged to him.

Just before six, Lucinda phoned her son with the thrilling news that someone had abandoned a '65 Buick on Thirtieth Street and she needed his help to lug car parts up to her studio. The auto was just the thing for making her largest Statue of Liberty yet, and wouldn't it be perfect to hook up one of the headlights to make a working torch?

"Yeah, Lucinda. Just perfect. I'll be home right after I check out Pete's new house." Rodent hung up and put his head in his hands. "Dragging the car up will be a piece of cake," he moaned. "But wait till she starts drilling on that metal. I have a headache just thinking about it."

"Headache?" said Mr. Harring, who had just arrived home and was making his way across the living room to his chair. "You don't know the meaning of the word, not until you have a four-hour meeting with Godfrey Naper. That man turned down every single idea my team came up with for his toilet paper." He sat down and let out a long sigh. "Peter, is it my imagination, or is your nose black-and-blue again?"

"Sort of." Peter tried to smile, but it hurt.

"Well," said Mrs. Harring, "shall we have dinner right away, Byron, so we can get down to the house while . . ."

"Scrull didn't send over the key," interrupted Mr. Harring.

"You mean we can't get inside the house?" wailed Erin. "I can't see the lab?"

"Rats!" said Rodent.

"How come?" asked Peter.

"Some delay with the transfer of the deed," said his father. "But the good news is that we might have electricity and water by moving day."

"You mean we might *not*?" said Peter.

"Oh, we probably will," said Mrs. Harring.

Not for the first time, Peter wondered about his mother's sanity. In the past she'd gotten more excited when he had an overdue library book than she was about moving sight unseen into a house that might or might not have a working toilet.

"Scrull said he'd try to get the key over to me first thing tomorrow," his father was saying.

"I was so hoping to take a look around tonight," said Mrs. Harring. "But at least we'll be settled in by the end of the month and the house will be ours."

"And not Cousin Rufus's," said Erin. "Right, Mom?"

Mrs. Harring smiled. "That's right, honey. Never Cousin Rufus's."

Fortified with three helpings of lasagna, Rodent went home to assist Lucinda with her Buick, and Erin and Peter were dismissed to their rooms to start packing.

Peter collapsed on his bed and thought about emptying out his closets and drawers, putting the things he no longer used into the box labeled GOODWILL and the things he wanted to take into the boxes marked TO MOVE, but he somehow could not summon the energy to begin.

"Peter?" Erin stepped into his room, holding a shopping bag. "Mom says I'm only allowed to take three of my collections, and she says not to take the birds' nests because I'll probably find more in the back yard, but I've used up all my boxes and I can't throw these out." She summoned her most pitiful expression. "Could you put them in your boxes?"

"Yeah, okay," said Peter. "But you pack them. I'm not getting blamed if they get mashed."

"Thanks!" Erin made a beeline for the nearest carton. "I owe you one." She sat down on the floor, took a nest from her bag, and began wrapping it with one of the sheets of newspaper that Mrs. Harring had put out for packing.

Peter watched her in silence as he petted his dog.

"You know," said Erin, "Pharaoh really looks Egyptian. He looks just like Anubis, the god of embalming."

From his position on the floor, Pharaoh turned one yellow eye toward Erin.

"Anubis was supposed to protect the dead, and maybe he did, because horrible things happened to archaeologists who opened some of the Pharaohs' tombs."

Peter did not want to know what horrible things, but Erin was already explaining.

"When King Tut's tomb was discovered, lots of people said there was a curse written on the door, but of course Howard Carter opened it anyway, and then this canary he'd bought for good luck got eaten by a poisonous snake." Erin placed her wrapped nest carefully at the bottom of the box. "And when the guy who put up the money for the excavation came to Egypt, he got bitten by a poison mosquito—"

"A poison *mosquito*?"

"Anyway, some kind of really infected insect bite killed him," said Erin as she began wrapping another nest. "And, at the very same second, back in England, his dog let out this awful howl and then dropped dead, too."

Erin went on to describe a wide variety of other mummies' curses, but Peter forced himself not to hear. What Nephia had called him, he told himself for the ninety-ninth time, did not sound like a curse.

But out the window, he knew, a half-moon hung in the twilight sky. It made him feel an urgency he could not explain. And if the full moon rose before he figured out what he was supposed to do, he had a feeling that something would happen, all right, and not something you'd throw a penny into a pool and wish for. But what? Nothing he'd come up with made any sense. There was only one thing he connected with full moons . . .

When the first ray of moonlight touched him, Harring the Daring began to change. Thick tufts of hair sprouted from his forehead, his chest, the backs of his hands. Two of his top teeth and two on the bottom lengthened into gleaming white fangs, sharp as ice picks. His throat was parched with a thirst that only blood could quench . . .

"What are you staring at my neck for?" asked Erin.

"Sorry," muttered Peter.

Erin held up a plastic storage container filled with disgusting brown-and-green goo in front of her brother's face. "Think I could put my bread-mold collection in one of your boxes?"

OUTSIDE THE PALACE, THE THIEVES BROKE INTO A RUN. THEY had done it! They had fooled the old witch! She never guessed that they had found their way into the Tomb of Cats and had searched until they had found a mummy just like the one they had stolen for her. Exactly the same!

Now the cat she coveted was theirs. Not that they understood its value. No, they knew only that if she wanted it so desperately, it must be worth far, far more than the golden treasures they had stolen from the tomb. And they had risked their necks to get it, had they not? Surely they should profit from their peril.

The stout thief had formed the plan. He reasoned that if the Pharaoh's sister knew the great value of the cat, surely others would know as well. They would whisper word of the little mummy into eager ears, they knew

the ones, and sell their treasure secretly to the highest
bidder.

But tomorrow would be soon enough to spread the
rumor. For now, the three headed for their hiding place,
where a jug of beer was waiting.

12

THE FOLLOWING AFTERNOON, RODENT, PETER, and Pharaoh waited on the corner to meet the Junior Scientists' camp bus. Finally, it arrived and Erin struggled off, holding a large piece of poster board.

"Tomorrow's the last day of camp," she said, "so we had to start bringing home our projects, and guess what? My chart on cow digestion won a blue ribbon. Did you know that cows have four stomachs?"

"Right, and two heads." Rodent carried Erin's camp bag up to the Harrings' apartment, while Peter held at arm's length a box with a faintly rancid odor, labeled COAGULATED PROTEIN.

Upstairs, Rodent flipped around the dial and found the 1933 version of *King Kong* on TV.

"You know what? King Kong was really only eighteen inches . . ."

"Shush, Erin!"

The three were still absorbed in the old movie when Mr. and Mrs. Harring came home from work.

Peter's father picked up the remote control and flicked off the set right in the middle of the scene where the great ape and Fay Wray had made it halfway to the top of the Empire State Building. He was greeted with a chorus of groans.

"This channel doesn't even show commercials," Mr. Harring complained. "Besides, who needs all that fantasy when we're having a real-life adventure!"

Peter was immediately wary. Once, his family had gotten stuck in the elevator in their building and had to be pulled out by their arms through a small doorway in the elevator's ceiling. He and Erin had been scared, but their parents acted extra-cheerful and told them they were having an adventure. When they used the word "adventure," they could mean anything.

Mr. Harring tossed something to his son. It was a key, brass and tarnished, with a circular handle and a long shaft ending in two squared-off teeth. As Peter examined it, Pharaoh got up from under the coffee table, where he'd been snoozing during the movie, and walked to his master's side.

"Tell them, Byron." Mrs. Harring was radiating happiness.

"Scrull sent over the key this morning," said her husband. "Your mother and I couldn't wait to see what the inside of the house was like, so we went downtown at lunchtime and had a tour."

"What's the laboratory like?" said Erin. "Are there test tubes and Bunsen burners and stuff all over the place?"

"I don't think Kathryn Coffin touched the lab after her father died," said Mrs. Harring. "And wait until you see the bedrooms! They're so spacious—there's even a spare one for you, Rode—and each one has a fireplace, and the kitchen has two stoves and . . .''

"But is it all cobwebby inside?" Erin asked. "Is it old and spooky and creaky?"

Mrs. Harring laughed. "Well, it is old, Erin, but the house is lovely. It's simply full of charm."

"And we met some of the Hell's Angels," said Mr. Harring. "Bones and what was that other one's name?"

"Lucifer, dear," said Mrs. Harring.

"That's right. Nicest guys you could hope to meet. They even offered to help us with the move." Mr. Harring rubbed his hands together. "Well, moving day's Saturday and are you kids going to be surprised!"

Peter handed the key back to his father. He bet that it was going to unlock quite a few surprises.

Mrs. Harring stayed home from work on Friday to finish the packing, and by Saturday morning everything was ready. The movers showed up, only forty-five minutes late, and as the last cartons were carried out of the apartment, Peter made a quick phone call to Rodent. "I thought you were coming over," he said. Then he had to hold the receiver slightly away from his ear until a loud jackhammer sound on the other end stopped.

"I was up until two last night helping with the jalopy," said Rodent wearily. "As soon as Szechuan Balcony opens for lunch, I'm hitting the hay." He sighed deeply. "Why couldn't Lucinda have studied accounting, like your mom, and be something normal?"

"Normal? Ha! Nothing around here is normal any-more, but anyway, come over tomorrow. First thing." And he gave Rodent the address.

When they had finished supervising the packing of the van, Mr. Harring hailed a pair of taxis. Mrs. Harring and Erin rode in the first, with shopping bags full of vases and crystal deemed too delicate for the movers to handle, and Peter, his father, and Pharaoh rode in the second. The movers promised they would be along right after they had some lunch.

When the two taxis arrived at the Coffin house, five formidable motorcycles were parked right in front.

"Isn't this great?" said Mr. Harring. "Lucifer told me that he and the boys would put their bikes here to save a space so the moving van can park." He gave one of the Harleys an affectionate pat and then opened the gate. "Come on, kids! Let's go inside."

Mr. Harring fitted the old brass key into the lock and the front door creaked open. The family stepped into the entryway. Dim light filtered in through the door; otherwise, the house was dark as pitch.

Mrs. Harring felt along the wall by the door for the light switch. She flipped it up and a chandelier blazed.

"Ho-ly cow!" exclaimed Erin.

They stood in the doorway to a large entry hall, its floor covered by a vast Oriental carpet. A stairway with an elaborately carved wooden banister swept up to the floor above. Tucked into its majestic curve was a grand-father clock, its hands stopped at two minutes to twelve. Beyond the clock, a wide hallway with doors opening off of it led to the rear of the house. But Peter noticed none of this. He saw only that on every wall, in even, vertical rows extending up to the ceiling, hung the mounted heads of leopards, lions, lynxes, and dozens of other big jungle cats, their mouths opened wide in silent roars.

"I mean, holy cat!" Erin corrected herself. Reverently, she approached a tiger. "This one's a Siberian. They're protected now, so this must be from a long time ago."

From his parents' hints, Peter had tried to picture what the inside of the Coffin house might be like, but even his vivid imagination had never conjured up anything like this. Beside him, Pharaoh was calm, showing no reaction to the fearsome felines.

"Aren't these heads wild?" Mrs. Harring advanced into the house, flinging open doors with delight, unveiling the parlor and the dining room, which adjoined the entryway hall. "Won't our friends simply be green with envy when they come over?"

Gray with grime was more likely, Peter thought.

As his mother closed the parlor door, a huge chunk of plaster fell from the hallway ceiling, barely missing her. "Oops!" she said, sidestepping the mess. "Well, we should expect to do a little repair work in a house this age. Now come down these stairs and see the kitchen. I can't wait to throw a dinner party!"

On the ground floor, Mrs. Harring behaved like a game-show hostess, exclaiming over outmoded laundry facilities, a sewing room, and, facing the rear of the house, a large old-fashioned kitchen. A single lion hung over the sink, a pair of leopards above the fireplace.

Peter felt certain that he was supposed to discover the treasure of Nephia's soul in this house. But where? Surely not someplace like the smelly old refrigerator his mother had just opened as if it were some coveted prize.

From the kitchen they went back up to the entry hall and began climbing the once-elegant curving staircase to the third floor, where the four main bedrooms were. As they ascended, the cat specimens were fewer and farther between, and seemed to get smaller, too, some as small as a common house cat, yet vicious in their frozen snarls. Mr. Harring gripped the banister only to have a large section of it come off in his hand. It seemed to Peter that the old house was doing its best to make them feel unwelcome.

But Mr. Harring didn't seem to notice. "Add carpenters to our list of people to phone on Monday, Jean," he said cheerily.

In the master bedroom, Mrs. Harring pulled up the shades to let in the light. "Maybe *New York* magazine will even want to do a little piece on 'The Harrings at Home,' " she said. "Isn't this lion over our fireplace splendid?"

Could this be his mother talking, Peter wondered. His mother, the conservationist, who had marched in front of Bergdorf's last winter carrying a leg-hold trap to protest the store's fur salon?

Erin said dibs on the room across the hall from her parents.

Peter peeked into the back bedroom next to Erin's. A panther hung over the fireplace and the room felt recently lived in. He walked over to the bed, which rested on a massive, dark wood frame with an ornately carved headboard depicting a knight slaying a dragon.

"This could have been Richard the Lion-Hearted's bed!" exclaimed Mr. Harring as he stepped into the room, followed by Erin.

"Byron?" came Mrs. Harring's voice. "What's wrong with this toilet?"

Mr. Harring hurried off to check.

"I bet Kathryn Coffin died here."

"Erin, do you enjoy being a ghoul?"

"I can tell. I wouldn't sleep in here for a million dollars."

Reaching for Pharaoh to bolster his courage, Peter sat down on the bed. "I'll do it for nothing," he said, staking his claim.

After adding plumbers to their list of people to call, the Harrings wove in and out of hallways, down narrow back stairs, into musty dressing rooms and out of dusty sitting rooms, exploring. All the while, Pharaoh stayed at Peter's heels like an odd, misshapen shadow.

On the fourth floor, Mr. Harring opened a glass-paneled door. "*Tah-dah!* The laboratory!" It was a large, circular room. Above and between its eight wide windows, which curved slightly with the arc of the room, hung dozens upon dozens of cat skulls.

Erin darted around checking out everything like a bargain hunter at a half-price sale. She sniffed at beakers dark with ancient residues and held cloudy test tubes up to the light. Blowing dust off a tarnished microscope, she removed a slide from its base and read the label.

"I knew it!" she cried. "Professor Coffin was a felid specialist!"

"A what?" asked her father.

"Cat expert," said Erin. "This is a cross section of a cat brain!" She put the slide back into place and squinted through the microscope's eyepiece. "Take a look!"

"Later," said Mr. Harring. "For now, let's keep going. I want you kids to see the whole house before the movers get here."

A warren of small rooms was on the fifth floor, and here the air was stale. "This is just the place for my study . . ." said Mr. Harring, opening a window. "Say, there's Bones." He stuck his head out. "Hey, Bones! Up here! It's me, Byron. Yeah! How's it going, man?"

Trying to ignore his father's jolly conversation with the biker, Peter wandered off down a hallway that ended beside a narrow door. He cracked it open, revealing wooden steps leading up. Attic steps. An apartment dweller all his life, Peter had never been in an attic, but he'd read enough about them in books to know that they were promising places for finding long-lost treasures.

"The movers are here!" Mr. Harring bellowed from somewhere below. "Everybody downstairs, on the double!"

Peter closed the door. But as soon as moving in was over, he planned to open it again.

TORCHES FLARED IN THE MOONLESS NIGHT AS A DOZEN SER-
vants of the Necropolis lifted Tachu's sarcophagus onto
the barge. No funeral procession attended her coffin.
No one wept.

Back on the riverbank stood the old Pharaoh, his
hands clasped behind his back. Nearby, two of Amenhut's servants shook their heads as the funeral barge
disappeared up the Nile. Never had they received or-
ders such as their master had given them. Never! Yet
there could be no doubt that the Pharaoh had found
the peculiar instructions among Tachu's scrolls. The
Pharaoh's sister did not wish to be mummified! No embalmer's knife had been allowed to cut out her liver,
her stomach, her intestines, her lungs. Even her brain
remained. Her body had been encircled in linen, but
no thick black pitch, symbolizing the vitality of the Nile
mud, had been painted over the wrappings. Rather, her
body had been packed into her mummy case with fine-

grained desert sand and an abundance of her talismans and charms. This had been her wish.

The servants shrugged. Although they would not speak of it to one another, each believed the sister of the Pharaoh had been an evil sorceress. If Anubis were to put her heart on a scale to be balanced by the Feather of Truth, they knew Tachu's heart would be heavy as stone. When a heart weighed more than the feather, Anubis would toss it to the beastly Gobbler, with the head of a crocodile, the forequarters of a lion, and the hind quarters of a hippopotamus, who lurked beneath the scale. And when the Gobbler swallowed a heart . . . *pif!* The seven spirits of that person ceased to exist. Perhaps it was this fate that Tachu sought to avoid with her odd burial plans. But not to be mummified! Unthinkable!

13

THE HARRINGS ALL JOINED IN TO DIRECT THE movers, scour the bathrooms, scrub floors, wipe cabinets, unpack cartons, and air out mattresses. Bones and a blonde he introduced simply as his motorcycle mama each carried in a box, poked around the house, and then lost interest. Even with their help, moving in took all day and then some. It was after ten o'clock that night when they finally sat down to supper from a nearby deli.

Mrs. Harring frowned across the big oak kitchen table at her son. Even discounting the bruises, fading reminders of Howie Krieger's right fist, his color wasn't good. "Honey, do you feel all right?"

"I'm just hungry," said Peter, and at the sight of the food he felt ravenous. He couldn't remember ever feeling as hungry as he'd felt these past few days. "Pass the pretzels, will you, Erin?"

"You know what? Food inspectors allow seventeen fruit-fly larva and one and a half maggots—"

"Erin . . ." warned Mr. Harring.

"—in a bag of pretzels."

"Guuuuph!" Peter spit his pretzel into a napkin.

"Oh, they won't hurt you. That's why they're allowed." Erin bit neatly into a pretzel to demonstrate.

Taking a deep breath, Peter made a conscious decision not to let his sister get under his skin. He had enough troubles as it was.

While the other members of his family slept soundly that night, Peter tossed and turned. He wasn't dwelling on the possibility that Kathryn Coffin had died in this bed, or on the ominous moans and whines of the old house. Something else kept sleep at bay, a hunch, a feeling that deep within this house something was stirring. Something he did not want to meet in the dark. Or even in broad daylight, for that matter.

Peter thought he knew why he was here. He had a job to do—all because of that dare of Rodent's he'd taken at the Met. But at least he was aware of the strangeness of the situation. Not like the rest of his family, who blithely accepted that they now lived directly across the street from a notorious motorcycle gang in a creepy old house with heads of dead animals decorating the walls.

In frustration, Peter tossed his pillow to the foot of his bed, next to where Pharaoh was curled. He laid his head on it, putting an arm around his dog. There was just enough moonlight to illuminate the odd carving on his headboard. The dragon had two heads, each breathing a tongue of flame, and a long, coiled tail. The knight, on horseback, had his arm drawn back and was just at the point of plunging his sword into the dragon's breast. But, Peter thought, as a wave of exhaustion washed over him, he'll never do it. He'll stay like that forever and he'll never slay the dragon.

At the first gray light of Sunday's dawn, Peter slid out of bed and threw on his clothes. Pharaoh stood at the side of the bed, ready and waiting.

"Come on, boy. Let's try the attic first. Maybe you can sniff out whatever it is I'm supposed to find."

In the morning light, the house seemed all the more cavelike and forbidding. Peter took several wrong turns before finding the staircase to the fourth floor, and became disoriented again looking for the attic door. When at last he found it, he took a deep breath as he twisted the knob. He didn't know what he'd find up here, but he hoped he'd find something.

It was dark above, and each step creaked slightly when Peter put his weight on it, but not loudly enough to wake anyone. Only holding on to Pharaoh kept him going.

At the top, strange, shadowy shapes loomed in the muted light coming up from the open door below. He took a deep breath and, with Pharaoh at his side, inched along, bumping into things, searching for a window. At last his hand felt the corrugation of a pair of shutters and, finding the latch, he opened them and then the dirty window. After doing the same with the second window, he had just enough light to survey the contents of the attic.

Something resembling a coffin stood upright in one corner, and in another, a phantom of a human shape, which turned out to be nothing more than a sewing dummy. Swallowing hard, Peter began his search.

But as the minutes passed and Peter opened old bureau drawers and sorted through steamer trunks, he found only everyday items—clothes flattened from being so long packed away, an umbrella, a carved pipe smelling still of aged tobacco, and curious metal instruments that, he imagined, must be the tools of a taxidermist. Nothing resembled a mummy's treasure.

Pharaoh did not sniff around the attic, coming up with a lead of his own. He merely stayed nearby, offering his calming presence.

Peter had just lifted the lid of an old hat box and found it filled with bundles of yellowed letters tied up with ribbons, when Rodent appeared at the top of the stairs. "Room service." He handed Peter a buttered bagel wrapped in a napkin. "Your mom sent this up. Man, I can't believe you *live* here, Pete! Across the street from a bunch of homicidal maniacs!"

Peter grinned. Reinforcements had arrived.

"Lucinda finished her Buick Liberty. She thinks it's her masterpiece, and I'm sprung for a couple of days, so here I am. Your mom had me stash my stuff in the room across the hall from yours, but I don't know if I can sleep here with those goons outside revving up their bikes." Rodent bit off a chunk of the bagel he'd brought up for himself. "What's with the cat heads, anyway?"

Peter shrugged as Erin's head popped up in the stairwell. "What're you doing up here, Peter?"

"Treasure hunting."

"Can I play?"

"I'm not playing," he said. "It's for real, and you'll just be in the way."

"Oh, come on, Pete. She can play." Rodent winked conspiratorially. "Here's what you do, Erin. Sit in this rocker and"—he picked up the hat box filled with letters—"read through these and see what clues you can find."

"Okay," said Erin, sorting through the nearly transparent sheets of paper. "Hey, these are from the Professor! Maybe there's stuff in here about his research." And she settled down to read while Rodent and Peter opened more dresser drawers, suitcases, and trunks, and sifted through their contents.

After nearly an hour, Peter stood up, rubbing the back of his neck to get the kinks out. "There's nothing up here that makes any sense." He walked over to one of the open windows.

Rodent shrugged and turned to Erin, who was still obediently reading. "Are those letters from old man Coffin?"

She nodded.

"So what'd he write home about?"

"Mummies."

Peter wondered if he was hearing voices again.

"Listen to this: 'My dear Clara, I pray that you and the children are well. I have been more fortunate in my search for the cat mummies of Ancient Egypt than I dared think possible.' "

"Erin—" Peter walked as calmly as he could toward his sister. "Give me that letter."

Erin shrugged her brother away. "When I'm finished."

But Peter couldn't wait. He scooted behind the rocking chair, where Rodent joined him, and, over Erin's shoulder, they read the spidery handwriting.

My first plans met with failure. The British Museum was not anxious to part with any of their specimens for a reasonable price, particularly when I explained what I had in mind. These museums! They merely display what they find and have contempt for scientists, such as myself, who are filled with the yearning for higher knowledge. When the curator there heard of my plan to unwrap the mummies to study the skulls of these ancient cats and compare them to our modern domestic felines, as well as to their larger, wilder kin, he bid me good day.

I believed then that it would be necessary for me to travel all the way to Egypt to secure the ancient skulls, and so I set out for the waterfront to book passage on a ship. At the pier, I found that the Delta Maiden *had docked the day before and was still unloading cargo from the voyage. Large crates labeled ''Bitumen'' were being hoisted to the dock. This aroused my scientific curiosity, since I knew of no bituminous fuel or coal natural to Egypt, so I strolled over to question one of the longshoremen about the crates. And, my dear Clara! These were his words! ''Ay, sir,'' he said, ''these here crates is full of bitumen, fuel or fertilizer, take yer pick. And this isn't the half of them, sir, not at all. There's nineteen tons of bitumen comin' off this ship. Yes, sir, it's nineteen tons of wee mummies those strange old Egyptian folk made out of their pussycats.''*

My darling Clara—can you imagine my ela-tion? On further inquiry of a shipping clerk, I was told that an enormous graveyard, filled only with mummies of cats held to be sacred to the Ancient Egyptians, had been excavated for ex-port to England. You see, my dear Clara, in time the inky pitch that those ancients used to preserve their dead turns to bitumen, an excel-lent fuel or fertilizer, just as the man said. My luck held and I was able to locate the gentleman in charge of receiving the shipment. With his permission, I checked into one of the crates and found that, though some of the outer linen of the mummies was damaged, the bodies were in-tact, and, most important for my purposes, their skulls were sound. So, dear Clara, I was able to purchase an entire crate of cats, more than enough for my study, for the price of coal!

Having obtained what I ventured out to find, I have now booked passage to New York on the Liberty, *and I shall return home to you before August ends.*

Give all the children a kiss for me.

Your loving husband,
Reginald

Rodent produced a low whistle. "Everywhere you go, Pete, it's mummies, mummies, mummies."

THE BOY STOOD NEAR THE GRAVE OF CATS, WATCHFUL IN the moonlight. Why had he listened to the old men, anyway? If that buffoon with the beer belly knew so much, would he have gotten his thieving hand sliced off? His was a foolish plan. It wasn't working. No one had come forward to offer gold for the mummy that the old crone had desired so fiercely. Oh, yes, the three of them had spread their rumor of a cat mummy worth a Pharaoh's treasure, but when they had told their wonderful secret, they had met with only scorn. Now they were the laughingstock of all the tomb robbers in the Necropolis!

The moon had been newborn when they had ransacked the Princess's tomb. Now it was nearly full, and still no one had come forward for the cat. He knew why: the *ka* of the Princess was already taking her revenge! Why had the old men not burned her mummy before they turned tail and ran?

The boy was all for giving up. They had their scarabs, didn't they? And the golden drinking cup, the bracelets, the necklaces? That was enough for him, but not for the old men. Oh, no. They were as greedy as they were cruel. Now they forced him to stand outside the Grave of Cats night after night, in case someone looking for a certain small mummy were to come to this desolate spot. Then he was to offer to sell the cat.

Well, he was sick of it! Holding the little bundle wrapped in coarse cloth close to his side, the boy darted into the cavernous entrance to the Grave of Cats. Along meandering pathways he scurried, his feet finding the way as the dim light faded to blackness. He had had enough of this troublesome mummy. Get rid of it, that's what he'd do, bury it so far back in the grave that it would disappear forever. He ducked under a toppled pillar too close to the ground for anyone but an agile boy to pass beneath. Here. This would do. Digging one hand into the nearest mound of cats, he lifted them and shoved Khaibit into their midst. Done! Brushing off his hands, he scuttled back the way he had come. He would simply tell the old men that the cat had been stolen and that would be the end of it. He spat on the ground. And good riddance, too!

14

HAVING RODENT AROUND GAVE ERIN SOMEONE to pester, leaving Peter free to mull over Professor Coffin's letter. It was an important piece of the puzzle, but what did it mean? Could one of the heads hanging on the walls be Nephia's cat? Could a cat be the treasure he was seeking? He spent Sunday afternoon wandering all through the house, returning each cat's glassy stare. But not one of them, nor the cat skulls in what they were already referring to as Erin's lab, seemed a likely candidate to be a mummy's treasure.

Both Peter's parents took Monday off from work. They continued to clean and unpack and organize with what Peter considered unnatural cheerfulness, and by that evening they declared they felt more or less settled.

On Tuesday morning, Mrs. Harring left for Bookworld before eight o'clock. With all the preparations for the move, she'd gotten behind at work and had to catch up. For the next few days, Mr. Harring intended to conduct business from the study he'd set up on the fifth floor so he could be home to deal with the plasterers, painters, and plumbers who were scheduled to come. But before he went upstairs, he gathered Peter, Rodent, and Erin together in the front parlor beneath the head of a puma. "Now listen to me, kids." He made eye contact with each of them, a technique he had learned at a weekend communications seminar. "I have got to work, work, work. I've promised Mr. Naper a new presentation by the end of the week, so I simply cannot, repeat cannot, be disturbed under any circumstances. Got it?"

"What about an emergency?" asked Erin. "Should we disturb you if there's an emergency?"

"Only an emergency of the most dire sort," he said, and disappeared up the stairs.

Erin and Rodent spent the morning in the lab. Peter was supposed to empty the dresser and closets in his room and put his clothes away, but he poked around in the attic instead, all the while turning Professor Coffin's letter every which way in his mind.

Around lunchtime, Mr. Harring slapped together bologna sandwiches and then he shooed the kids and dog outside. "Since we have a back yard, you might as well take advantage of it." As he handed Peter his lunch, he added, "And you look as if you could use a dose of sun and fresh air, young man."

Peter didn't think a totally tree-shaded back yard in the middle of a smog-infested city was exactly a prescription for good health, but he ate his sandwich sitting in one of the uncomfortable porch chairs made of bent tree boughs with the bark still attached. Erin and Rodent were discussing whether one did or did not have taste buds on the bottom of one's tongue, and Peter wondered if maybe he should ask his sister to come in at bedtime and talk to him about her scientific theories. It certainly was putting him to sleep right now.

"I'm going in to catch a few Z's," he announced. He clicked to Pharaoh and the dog followed him inside. But by the time he got up to his bedroom, the sleepiness had passed.

Instead of napping, he started hunting again. When the dresser drawers revealed large and mysterious undergarments which he could not bring himself to touch, he simply pulled one of the emptied packing boxes up next to the dresser and slid out the drawers. Soundlessly, he poured unmentionables, balled-up stockings, flannel nighties, and the like into the box, but nothing unusual toppled out with them. Peter then searched the drawer in a bedside table and found hairpins and large, decorative combs. The matching table on the other side of the bed contained just stationery and medications, including a small bottle of Ajax Aspirin.

Discouraged, Peter collapsed across his bed. Sir Knight hadn't yet slain the dragon on his headboard, but he was better off than Sir Harring de Daring, who hadn't even found his dragon. Behind the knight stood a carved castle with towers and turrets and even a moat and a drawbridge. Peter scooted up and knelt in front of the headboard, running his hand over the carving. It was certainly dusty enough to have been around since the time of Richard the Lion-Hearted. Strange, though, the way the drawbridge stuck out from the gatehouse. Peter's fingers probed and at last felt what he suspected he might feel: hinges. Using the edge of a quarter, Peter worked and pried along the sides of the drawbridge until—bingo! He opened the door, revealing a secret compartment inside the headboard, a niche about the size of a shoe box. And Kathryn Coffin had filled it up with marbles, little tin animals, a jump rope, and unfinished needlework with wobbly stitches spelling out COME WHEN YOU ARE CALLED. Finally Peter pulled out a small green leather book marked with a purple ribbon.

So intent was he on his find that Peter hardly heard the doorbell chime or his father call, "Coming!"

Mr. Harring raced downstairs, but stopped short outside Peter's room. "I thought I told you kids to go outside."

"Had to get something," mumbled Peter, following his father down the stairs.

"I hope this is the plumber," said Mr. Harring, opening the front door. "Hey, Bones! Oh, nothing much. Sure, you can borrow a beer. Come on in."

"What's that?" Erin wanted to know when Peter stepped out the kitchen door to the porch where she and Rodent were sitting.

"Just an old book."

Erin went back to telling Rodent how vampire bats have to drink half their body weight in blood every night, so Peter could read in peace, without further questions. He sat down, with Pharaoh at his feet, and opened the little volume. It was Kathryn Coffin's girl-

hood diary, as he had guessed. He flipped through it
and fragments of the brown-edged pages flew out.

Beginning with the first entry, dated New Year's Day
1913, Peter started reading. He read about Elizabeth,
Kathryn's new china-headed doll with real human hair,
about the day her father returned from a long journey,
about the thrill of a train trip to New Orleans. He read
of the day Kathryn was scolded for ruining her stockings
helping the gardener set out the new rosebushes, of a
shopping expedition for an Easter bonnet. Page after
page he read, slowly and thoroughly. Just as he was
beginning to doubt that he would find anything helpful
between the covers of Kathryn's diary, he turned the
page and read:

April 17

Dear Diary,
Tonight I crept up to the laboratory and stole—
yes, stole!—a mummy from my father's crate of
cats, the one I call Goldie. His sweet sad face is
too fine to be destroyed, and so I rescued him.
My heart still thumps from my deed, and yet I
cannot believe that I did wrong. My father has
so many cats I do not think he would mind that
I took the one with the green eyes that seem to
look out at me with such longing. I wrapped
Goldie in Elizabeth's second-best blanket, the
blue one, and buried him tonight by the light of
the full moon in the big hole that Wilbur has
dug to plant the new sycamore. I hope he will
rest peacefully there.

Peter stopped reading. He'd seen a pair of green cat eyes. They'd looked out at him from the top of Nephia's mummy case. Now the pieces of the puzzle that had been free-floating in his brain for the past few days were snapping together, making sense. "Pharaoh," he whispered, "is that it? Nephia wants her cat back?"

The dog got to his feet.

"Erin," Peter said, "is one of these trees a sycamore?"

"That one." Erin pointed to the tree on the right side of the yard. "See how its bark peels off on the branches? That's how you can tell. The other one's a maple. Its leaves have five points."

Peter walked slowly toward the massive sycamore. Its mottled branches rose skyward, leafing out and shading the yard.

"What're you doing?" Erin scampered after Peter and Pharaoh.

Rodent was not far behind. "The tree didn't start talking to you, did it, Pete?"

Peter tried to imagine this giant as a newly planted sapling with a little cat mummy tucked in among its roots. He wondered whether the mummy could have survived. It had survived for three thousand years before its burial here, but still . . .

"Okay, Pharaoh. Let's see what you can do with those big paws of yours, boy. Dig up what I need, boy. Dig!" And Pharaoh began scratching away the earth beneath the tree.

Erin's eyes widened. "I'm telling."

"Go ahead."

Erin began trotting toward the house.

"I'm sure Dad will think this is a big emergency."

Erin made it all the way to the screen door before she changed her mind. "Okay, okay," she said, returning to the back yard, "but you have to tell me what's going on!"

"It's . . . complicated" was all Peter could say.

Half in the dark himself, Rodent came to the rescue. "It's still the treasure hunt," he explained. "Only now we're pretending that Pharaoh's digging for a mummy's treasure. You know how those old Egyptians always had all that gold and stuff, and after he finds it, we're going to fill in the hole, split the loot, and be the richest kids in New York."

"Can I keep playing?"

"Sure." Rodent waggled his eyebrows at Peter. "In fact, we're even going to let you get a shovel and help ol' Pharaoh out."

"Thanks!" said Erin. "I know where a shovel is." She scampered over to the cellar doors.

"No, Erin!" called Peter. "Don't go down there!"

But Erin had already pulled one of the heavy doors open and Rodent was striding over to the dark rectangle. Peter ran after them.

The three of them stood on the top stair. Peter wrinkled his nose against the odor and reached down for Pharaoh, forgetting that the dog was no longer at his side.

"*Sheesh!*" said Rodent, backing up a step. "I have a feeling I wouldn't be the only rodent down there. And, hey, what if a couple of Hell's Angels are using this place to hide out from the cops?"

"I'm not scared," said Erin. "I go down there all the time since I started my spider collection."

Peter swallowed. If Erin could do it, he could, too. He had to put the brakes on his imagination or he'd go crazy. It was just a smelly old basement, and that was all.

"No, I will," Peter said, and without stopping to think, he plunged down into the cellar, holding his breath, as if he were jumping into a bottomless pool of dark water. He tripped on the last step, stumbling in the blackness. And then through the gloom he felt a force, a vast swell of negative energy that was pushing, pulsing, breaking into this place. As he sensed the forming power, he knew, without knowing how, that it had something to do with Nephia and with him—that he, Harring the Daring, had been brought here to reckon with whatever evil might spill out into his world from this ominous rip in the void.

Peter waved his hands wildly above his head for the pull string for the light. There! But in the glow from the low-watt bulb he saw, as before in the dark he had only felt, a jagged crevice splitting the cellar wall.

THE KNEES OF THE CHIEF TOMB GUARD RATTLED TOGETHER with fear as he told the aged Pharaoh of his discovery. Nephia's burial chamber had been violated!

At first, Amenhut refused to believe this dreadful news. But not many hours after the guard left his chamber, he summoned his priests. If Nephia's tomb had been robbed, he told them, they must replace all that had been taken. His beloved daughter must lack nothing in the Land of the Dead.

Now many torches burned in holders along the stone walls of the Princess's burial chamber, casting a glimmering yellow light. A priest wearing a leopard skin wound fresh, bright linen around Nephia's small body. A priest in a jackal mask stood nearby, handing him stones and precious gems to slip inside the wrappings. One more scarab, one more jewel, and they were finished. The priests then gently laid Nephia's body back inside her mummy case. Their work complete, they bowed to the Pharaoh.

Amenhut stepped forward. Once straight and tall, he was now stooped with age and sorrow. How he missed his loved ones who had so early joined the host of stars lighting the nighttime sky. The Pharaoh's face showed his anguish, his outrage at the violation. His daughter's games, her golden bracelets, her drinking cup—these had been easy to replace. But why had the thieves stolen her cherished Khaibit? What use could they have for the mummy of a cat?

Sighing, Amenhut reached out a hand and stroked the painted cheek of the face that was once his lovely girl, touched her lacquered hair. Then the God-King stepped back and, with a resigned gesture, signaled two servants who stood waiting. The servants put on the lid of the inner mummy case. Then from the shadows of the tomb came two priests with lion masks and skins of lions down their backs. They strode to Nephia's coffin and stood one on each side. Raising their hands in prayer, they chanted to Osiris to accept once more the *sahu* spirit of Nephia into his kingdom of the Shining Ones. They implored him not to let her seven spirits wander in Amenta, ghostly and alone. They prayed that her tomb be sealed evermore from thieves who would plunder her treasures. The lion priests held high a bowl of fragrant, smoking liquid. Using a brush made from the finest gazelle hair, they painted the smoldering mixture where the lid rested on the base of the coffin. With this potion and with their powerful prayers from the Forbidden Scroll, they sealed Nephia's casket against evil intrusion.

When the lion priests had finished, they placed the inner mummy case into one just slightly larger. This they put into another, bigger case, and then lifted these into a coffin covered with a layer of hammered gold. Two more priests came to aid their brothers as they lowered the nested cases into the stone sarcophagus. Then they fitted on the heavy lid. Chanting slowly, the priests led the way out of the tomb. More slowly, Amenhut followed, glancing back longingly at Nephia's coffin. Then, setting his face to hide his heartache and holding his head erect, he stepped through the door. The servants removed the torches from their holders along the wall and walked behind the Pharaoh out of the tomb.

15

 "WHAT ARE YOU, CRAZY?" RODENT WAS sprawled on the ground and Peter sat nearby, panting.

"Peter! What happened?" Erin sounded frightened. "Why did you come up the stairs like that?"

"Ran right over me!" Rodent sat up, rubbing his shoulder. "Like a Mack truck!"

"It's just—"

"Just what?" Rodent stood, brushing dirt from his clothes.

"Nothing." Peter'd started to say that there was something down there, something awful. But now, out in the daylight, he half doubted that there had been.

"You had me scared for a minute," said Erin. "And, hey, you didn't get me a shovel."

"The shovel's too heavy for you." Peter forced himself to return to the cellar entrance. "Maybe you can find a nice big stick to dig with." As Erin raced off, he closed the doors and sat down on top of them. "Rode, do me a favor. Get my bike lock, will you? My bike's in the laundry room."

"What do you want *that* for?"

"Just get it, okay?"

When Rodent returned with the lock, Peter wound the chain three times through the handles of the cellar doors and snapped it shut. He doubted that it would help much if whatever was down there truly wanted to get out, but it was all he could think to do. Then he went and sat with Rodent under the maple, and watched Pharaoh. The dog had made some real progress on his dig. At the bottom of a bathtub-sized hole, he was clawing dirt away underneath the arc of a large root close to the base of the tree.

Erin had found a pointed stick and was happily digging for the mummy's treasure beside the dog. "I know how the Egyptians made mummies," she said as she bored her stick deeper into the dirt. "See, when someone died, he'd be taken to the Necropolis, which was the City of the Dead, and his corpse would be laid out on a table and an embalmer would cut open the left side of the abdomen." Erin stood up and pointed out the exact spot on her own abdomen. "Then the embalmer would reach in and pull out the lungs, stomach, intestines, and liver, and put them in jars. And you know what? They didn't understand what the brain was for, so they just threw it away, but you know how they got it out of the skull?"

"No," said Rodent.

"They'd take this long, curved hook and stick it up the dead person's nose into a hole in the skull and poke it all around to chop up the brain and break it into little mushy pieces."

"Gross!" said Rodent.

"Then they'd take these teeny tiny spoons with long handles and stick them up through the nose and spoon out all the little globs of brain. Or, if they mashed it up enough, they'd just turn the corpse over and his brains would run out his nose."

Peter decided against leaving that note about being turned into a mummy.

As Pharaoh dug deeper and deeper beneath the tree, Erin went on to lecture about how embalmers sprinkled natron crystals, which were like grains of salt, onto the hollowed-out corpse and left it on the table for forty days and all the fluids in the body would, as she put it, *drip, drip, drip*. She told how next the body cavity was perfumed and stuffed with cloth to fill it out, and how the mummy got fake stone eyes for seeing in the Land of the Dead. Then the body was wrapped in linen strips, with lots of charms tucked in to protect the dead person, and a priest would paint the mummy with pitch. "It was thick and gooey, like tar," Erin finished up. "I hate to be sticky, don't you?"

All the time she talked there in the old steep-walled garden, Pharaoh dug, but nothing other than soil and a tangle of tree roots showed inside the hole.

The vigil over the digging continued throughout the afternoon, until that evening, when they were called in to dinner. Erin and Rodent hurried into the kitchen, but Peter stopped at the screen door and looked back into the yard. In the twilight, the overgrown garden had a mysterious quality, and there beneath the sycamore was the biggest mystery of all. Pharaoh wasn't visible now, but a spray of dirt could be seen coming from the hole as regularly as a heartbeat, and Peter felt a tremendous surge of love for this tireless digger.

"Come in, Peter," called his mother. "Your dinner's getting cold."

He opened the screen door, thinking that it was a stroke of good fortune, or perhaps some supernatural plan, that his parents had never once strolled out into the yard.

That night, a nearly round moon inched across the sky—a moon bright enough so that Peter, as he sat on the largest of the dirt mounds that Pharaoh had created with his digging, cast a shadow. Forcing his tired eyelids up each time they lowered dangerously, he made himself stay awake, on guard. And if something did creep up, out of that cellar, well, he wasn't sure what he'd do, but at least Pharaoh wouldn't be alone.

"Let me get my facts straight," Rodent had said when he and Peter were getting ready for bed. "When everyone's asleep, you're going to sneak outside to protect your dog from some evil force? Is that right?"

Peter nodded.

"Pete, you got it backward. Dogs are supposed to protect their masters."

But Peter couldn't bear the thought that something might happen to Pharaoh. After much persuasion, Rodent had promised to come outside with him, but by the time Mr. and Mrs. Harring and Erin had turned off their lights, Rodent was snoring, and Peter decided to let him sleep. His jitters over the Hell's Angels would just drive him crazy anyway, and so, after borrowing Erin's flashlight, Peter had come outside alone.

All through that long night, when each minute seemed an hour, he sat on the edge of the hole while the dogged dog dug deeper and deeper beneath the tree. Just as Peter was beginning to believe he could stay awake no longer, just as the sky began to lighten in the east, Pharaoh bounded out of the pit and nudged him with his nose.

"What's up, boy?"

At first it was hard to see amid the interweaving of roots, but then something reflected the flashlight's beam. He slid down into the hole, feet first, scrambling over protruding parts of the tree. At the bottom he found that, sure enough, Pharaoh had uncovered a small trunk, a miniature of the kind he'd seen people in old movies take on long sea voyages. The rotted leather strap snapped in his hand as Peter pulled on it, but by prodding with the toe of his sneaker, he was able to loosen the trunk from the ground. He tucked it under one arm and climbed awkwardly up.

He set the trunk down on the grass. Pharaoh paced nervously around it. With a stick, Peter pried up the two rusted metal clasps on its front. Holding the flashlight between his knees, he raised the lid. His head began to tingle as he lifted out a hard, oblong object wrapped, as the diary entry had said it would be, in an old blue blanket, somehow not much the worse for age. Gingerly, he unwound the coverlet, and found himself holding the mummy of Nephia's cat.

NEPHIA WANDERED IN THE FIELDS OF PEACE ALONE NOW. THE little spirit, as much a part of her as her own *khaibit*, was missing. She had appealed to the gods to help return him to her, but without Khaibit's mummy in the coffin beside her own, they could do nothing.

Nephia's seven spirits did return to visit her mummy, but they plucked no plump red grapes adorning the tomb wall. No rendering of bread nourished them, nor sweetly painted figs, nor melon. Without the comfort of their small, four-legged companion, they had no appetite.

In the Land of the Living, the centuries marched by and at last Maat's prophecy was fulfilled. The kiss! How it startled her! But quickly she had found her voice to tell him of his task. Then, through the Eye of Horus, she had watched her man of the future with his pale skin and his strange bushy hair the color of a copper pot! Yes, she had spoken once, and after his protector had arrived, she spoke a second time. Maat had said: *Speak thrice; he shall hear you.* She might speak just once more to this man who now held her cherished Spirit-cat! What words should she choose to bring her sweet Khaibit back into her arms?

16

As peter pulled the blue blanket from the treasure, Pharaoh sat next to him, entranced. For the first time since the dog had appeared in the taxi, his wide yellow eyes were not sad or worried, but shone with an eager light.

Peter held the flashlight steady on the cat. Its wrappings formed a pattern of rectangles, like dozens of little doorways. The linen wrappings were a dark shade of gold and the cat's face a lighter gold, with eyes, nose, mouth, and whiskers marked in black line. It had small painted eyebrows and its ears pointed up, alert, as if it were listening still. Pharaoh raised a stately forepaw and placed it, just for a second, on the mummy.

Now what? Even though he had managed to find Nephia's treasure, he wasn't at all sure he'd be able to bring it back to her before the moon grew full. Lost in these thoughts, Peter never heard the snapping of a twig or a rustle in the grass if, in fact, such sounds were made. Rather, it was the feeling of being watched that made him turn around and aim his feeble flashlight beam upward. There, standing close beside him, was a tall woman in red.

Rodent had been right! Someone had been hiding in the cellar and now she'd come out! Was one of the Hell's Angels close behind?

Peter dropped the flashlight. But in the moonlight the woman's expectant face, surrounded by dark, heavy hair, was all too visible. Her almond-shaped eyes were outlined in thick black makeup, and her lips, painted red, formed a smile. Her strange appearance and the snake-headed bracelets winding up her arms from her elbows to her shoulders made Peter suspect that this might not be a biker woman.

She made no move toward Peter. Her eyes flicked from him to the mummy as she raised one hand to her throat to grasp a blue pouch dangling from a delicate chain.

Peter struggled to his feet. Holding the little mummy close, he began backing away. Pharaoh did the same, keeping between him and the stranger.

Inside his head, Peter began to experience a loud crackling, like harsh static, and then a low, throaty voice broke through the noise. *"I have come to help you, man of the future."*

Peter's head throbbed. He shifted the cat to his other arm and his mind formed a question of its own. "Who are you?"

The woman's lips remained smiling. *"I am the* ka, *the twin spirit, of Tachu."*

Peter dimly remembered the guide at the museum talking about a *ka* spirit. And her name, Tachu, he had heard before.

"Princess Nephia was Tachu's niece," she told him. *"I, Tachu's ka, have come to help you fulfill Maat's prophecy."*

"Prophecy?" thought Peter.

"It is written that Maat, goddess of justice and truth, will send one to avenge the spirits of Nephia. You are the one."

Somehow Peter was not surprised.

"Ah, yes. Give the cat to me now and your job will be finished. I will take care of everything."

Peter crouched down beside Pharaoh. He put his free arm around him, hoping for a clue as to what he should do, but the dog's eyes remained fastened on the woman.

"This creature can tell you nothing. He will be of no further use to you."

He is mine to command, thought Peter, and as he stood once more, he realized that not only could the *ka* put words into his mind but she could read it as well.

"Why do you want to help?" Peter managed. If it made sense to him, maybe he would hand over the little mummy. He certainly had no idea how to get it back to Nephia.

The *ka* seemed to sigh. *"In life, Tachu was possessed by demons of evil. Jealousy of her brother the Pharaoh Amenhut withered her heart."*

Now Peter remembered her face. At the Met—she was the one they'd called Old Evil Eyes!

"Ambition for the throne of Egypt gnawed like a rat at her soul and she plotted her brother's death. But Nephia got in her way and Tachu never had a second chance."

The *ka* paused, as if it was painful to continue.

"For three thousand years I, the ka, *and the other spirits of Tachu have suffered the tortures of the damned."*

Peter's head ached from the flood of words, and still they poured in.

"We, her spirits, have never been allowed to enter the Land of the Dead. Rather, we are without a resting place." The *ka* moaned sadly.

She was quite ghostly now except for the small blue pouch at her throat. It alone remained substantial. But as this thought entered his mind, the *ka* groped for the pouch, and grasping it, she became solid once more.

"Through the prophecy of Maat, Tachu has received a chance—one chance!—to escape this eternity of suffering! I, the ka, *have come to rectify the long-ago evil. I want only to return Khaibit to Nephia."*

Khaibit. So that was the cat's name.

"Once the good is done, Tachu can enter the Land of the Dead and she will be at peace, at peace, at peacccce . . ."

Hissing sounds swirled in Peter's head. He supposed that what the *ka* had said made sense. After centuries of paying for her crimes on earth, Tachu desperately needed this one chance to do good so that she could enter the Land of the Dead. She wanted to return the cat to Nephia, and if the *ka* only wanted to do what he was to do, why not let her?

The *ka* smiled, as if pleased with the course of Peter's thoughts.

What a relief to stop hearing voices, to stop trying to puzzle out what to do, to live strictly in the present.

Slowly, Peter held out the cat to Tachu's *ka*.

FOR TACHU, THE JOURNEY TO THE HALL OF TWO TRUTHS HAD not been particularly perilous. The beastly gatekeepers inhabiting the nether realms were, after all, the dark powers she had called upon time and again while in the Land of the Living. When she reached the Hall, it came as no surprise that the weight of her wicked heart nearly toppled Anubis' scale. But just as the jackal-headed god picked up her heart to throw it to the Gobbler, Tachu began to chant. Her words wove a spell of such power and magic that, instead of being devoured, Tachu's heart found its way back into her body. The incantation had worked! She was free of the Gobbler! Free, free, free!

But . . . where *was* she? To her left, a lake of fire crackled with a choking stench. To her right came an army of scorpions. And behind her a reptile with seven heads and teeth like iron prongs snapped at her heels. This was not a Field of Peace. No, this was some hellish mistake. She was in Amenta, Place of Outer Darkness, where the gloom became so thick one could touch it. Alas! Tachu had no spells left. She had only the blue pouch containing every ingredient for the Potion of Eternity—save one. And without that one element, it might as well be the Potion of Pointlessness, for all the good it did her.

Gradually, it dawned on Tachu that her *sahu* and the seven spirits it contained were condemned forever to wander these murky depths that were neither here nor there. The pain! The utter exhaustion! Had she but known what awaited her, she herself would have thrown her heart into the Gobbler's maw!

Oh, to sit, just for a moment. But even slowing down invited the snip of teeth as sharp as daggers. She must keep moving, though thorns pierced her feet and claws of winged beasts tore at her gown. Was there no chance for her, none at all?

Ah, perhaps. Her brother's message from Maat. Could she believe she was the Old One referred to in the prophecy? The one that Set, god of the dark, would send to battle against Maat's man of the future? She could. She did. It wasn't much comfort, yet it provided Tachu with a glimmer of hope.

From his gloomy domain of eternal night, mule-headed Set observed Tachu in her misery. Although he could have ended her suffering at any time, he did not lift a finger to do so, for he well understood that centuries of torture would strengthen her resolve to return to earth, seeking everlasting life. Tachu would lead the way to the Land of the Living, open the portal, and then his legions would follow.

And when at last three thousand years had slipped away and the time had come for the fulfillment of Maat's prophecy, Set watched as Tachu's *ka* separated from her *sahu*; he looked on as Tachu unfastened the golden chain from her own neck and hung the priceless pouch around the neck of her twin. He followed the progress of the *ka* as she navigated the difficult passage from the dead lands to the Land of the Living. He kept his eyes on her as she hid in the darkness, waiting, waiting to grab her chance at immortality.

Not once did Set glance back at Tachu's *sahu* in Amenta. It did not interest him to see the afflicted creature staggering about, with the fetid breath of the seven-headed reptile scorching the back of her neck.

17

As PETER EXTENDED THE CAT MUMMY TOWARD the *ka*'s eager hands, he glanced down at its small, painted-on face and saw something—perhaps what Kathryn Coffin had seen all those years ago. The something that had caused her to choose *this* mummy from among hundreds to rescue from her father's lab.

Peter hesitated. "I . . . I have to think about it."

"I can wait," said the *ka*. *"I have waited for centuries. I can wait yet a few minutes more."* Again she brought her fingers to the blue pouch at her throat. *"But the disk of the moon grows round and time grows short."*

"Why?" said Peter. "What will happen at the full moon?"

A smile flitted over the *ka*'s lips. *"It is written that the man of the future must return Khaibit to Nephia between the new moon and the full one. And if he fails, he will become''*—her stare hardened—*''. . . a man of the past.''*

A cold chill traveled down Peter's spine. "What does that mean?"

"Give me the cat and you need not worry further."

All this time, while the *ka* spoke and Peter listened, Pharaoh had pressed against his legs. The dog's eyes shone with a fierce, pleading gaze.

The *ka* held out her hand. The patience of three thousand years was wearing thin. *"Give me the Spirit-cat now!"* All pretense of charm was fading. *"I must have the Spirit-cat!"*

She had betrayed herself. Peter took a step back, and then another. He had to get away. Securing the cat under his arm like a football, he turned and ran from the figure in red, unaware of Pharaoh at his heels, keeping between him and the *ka*. He ran in a zigzag path past the old birdbath, toward the house. But when he stopped to catch his breath, there was the *ka* before him! The house seemed far away.

The twin spirit threw back her head and laughed. Her gaping mouth revealed gums studded with only the stump remains of teeth, as the horrid cackle invaded Peter's thoughts.

"O Maat!" she cried. *"Can this simpleton really be the man of the future? The one awaited for centuries?"* The *ka* shot out a long finger, pointing it at the dog, and angry syllables erupted. *"Tataui sat em dati!"*

Pharaoh never wavered.

Bending toward the dog and squinting in the gray light of dawn, the vile thing dropped her hand. *"Curse the Eye of Horus!"* And a terrible pain gripped Peter's head. He felt as if his skull was being squeezed in a vise. *"Give me the cat! I must have its knucklebone!"*

"Pharaoh!" Peter cried, wanting to thrust the cat away. "Stop her!"

The dog seemed to grow even as he received Peter's command. His eyes, now gleaming with a fierce red spark, locked with those of the *ka*, and the pressure in Peter's head diminished. A tremor shook the ground. The leaves overhead quivered and the very sky above thundered with the enormous clash of opposing wills. Peter suddenly felt a small and insignificant part of what was surely an ancient battle.

Suddenly, he glimpsed a face on the back porch. Rodent!

Peter knew he would be finished if he let the *ka* get into his mind again. "Rode!" He faded back. "Here comes the bomb!"

The mummy twirled through the air.

"Peter?" It was Erin, not Rodent.

"Pharaoh!" Peter cried desperately. "Get the cat!"

Lightning cracked in the sky as ropes of sparks surrounded the *ka*. Inside his head, Peter heard her anguished scream as the dog leaped up, up to the little mummy arcing in the air. Opening wide his jaws, Pharaoh caught the cat with the same ease with which he had once caught the Frisbee. On the ground again, he raced into the house, past Erin, who still stood by the open door.

"Peter? What are you doing out there?" Erin let the door shut behind her as she padded across the porch and down the steps.

Peter didn't answer. The space where the *ka* had been entrapped inside the coil of sparks was now only a fading red silhouette of a figure, as if an array of bright flashbulbs had exploded.

Shakily Peter walked toward the house. A few steps away from the porch, he spotted his bike lock lying on the ground. He picked it up and found that the chain had been snapped in two. Over at the corner of the house, the cellar doors were flung wide open.

It was dark in the tomb of Amenhut, but the spirits needed no light as they hovered above the great stone sarcophagus that contained the Pharaoh's mummy.

His *ka* was there, a mirror image of Amenhut in his eighty-fifth and last year in the Land of the Living; and the *ren*, the secret name. True was the *ab*, the heart, and mighty the *sekhem*, the power-spirit. Still quick was his wit, his *khu*. The shadow-spirit, Amenhut's *khaibit*, flitted about the tomb, partaking of the vast array of funeral offerings.

Six were there in the tomb.

But where was the Pharaoh's *ba*, his eternal soul? Where was this shape-changer that could pass from the Land of the Dead to the Land of the Living as easily as a man can pass from one room of a house to another?

Six were there in the tomb. One was missing.

18

"A MUMMY?" ASKED ERIN, INCREDULOUSLY, AS a not quite awake Rodent joined the Harrings at the breakfast table. "A mummy buried in our back yard?"

Peter slumped farther down in his chair, exhausted. When he'd come in from the back yard, Erin had been right behind him, asking a million questions. He'd managed to put her off while he searched for Pharaoh, swearing to tell all after he checked on his dog. He'd finally found him curled up under his bed, the mummy resting between his paws.

Whatever had happened out there in the night had weakened Pharaoh greatly. He didn't respond when Peter crawled halfway under the bed to stroke his back and talk soothingly to him, but he did blink when Peter touched the cat. Sensing that there was little he could do to speed the dog's recovery. Peter merely scooted the mummy closer to Pharaoh's chest.

Back in the kitchen, he tried again to explain. "I watched Pharaoh dig all night, and then the twin spirit of this really evil ancient Egyptian showed up, and she had all these bracelets with snake heads . . ."

"What a horrible nightmare!" Mr. Harring lifted a stack of bowls from an overhead cabinet. "Who's ready for oatmeal?"

"Dad, it wasn't a nightmare, it was . . ."

"You know, I think you've been coming down with something for the last few days." Mrs. Harring put a hand to her son's forehead. "You feel very warm, Peter."

"You'd feel warm, too, if some evil sorceress was after you!" Frantically, Peter turned to his sister. "You saw her!"

Erin shook her head. "I woke up hungry, and came downstairs and heard you yelling bloody murder and the next thing I know Pharaoh practically knocks me over running into the house and you're walking around the yard like a zombie." She reached for the sugar. "There wasn't anybody out there but you, Peter."

Mrs. Harring blotted her lips on a napkin. "Well, I've got to get to the office, but first I'm taking my eldest child up to bed." Gently, she pried Peter out of his chair. "Anybody know if we've unpacked the thermometer?"

"Mom, I'm not sick," objected Peter. "It was all a bad dream. Boy, what a terrible dream! But now it's over and I've got to go up to the Met today and . . ."

"You are going nowhere, Peter, and that's final." Mrs. Harring put an arm around her son and escorted him upstairs. She made him put on his pajamas and brought him extra pillows. Then she pulled the covers up to his chin. "A full day of bed rest will fix you up." She kissed him on the forehead. "Feel better. I'm off."

As soon as his mother left the room, Peter peeked under the bed. Pharaoh was still there, sleeping deeply. How he wished that he, too, could sleep. How he wished that bed rest really could fix him up. Well, it was only Wednesday, and the full moon wasn't until Friday night . . .

Peter allowed his eyes to close.

"Pssst, Peter!" Erin stood beside his bed. "Are you asleep?"

"Not anymore."

Rodent appeared at his doorway. "Erin, I told you not to come in here."

"You're not the boss of me." Erin turned to Peter. "So let's have it," she said. "The whole story."

Peter sighed and pulled himself to a sitting position. "Only if you swear just to listen for once in your life and not say a word."

Erin drew a zipper across her lips and seated herself on Peter's bed. Rodent took a chair by the window.

"About two weeks ago, Rodent and I were in the Met, trying to find this mummy's toe . . ." Peter began. He told of sneaking into the gallery and of Princess Nephia's mummy case. As he described her face, so small, so delicate, with her mysterious smile, he pictured her clearly in his mind.

"Go on," said Erin.

Peter hadn't realized that he'd stopped. He told then

how Rodent had dared him to touch Nephia's mummy mask, but how, instead, he'd kissed it.

"You *kissed* a mummy?"

"Erin . . ."

"Sorry, sorry. Go on."

He told how Nephia had spoken to him, saying that the dog was his to command until the full moon. "And after that, it's too late for me to give the cat back." Another chill passed through Peter. He kept talking, hoping it would go away. As he told how the eye on the golden collar was like the Eye of Horus at the Met, Erin's own eyes were wide. He finished finally with the appearance of the woman in red. Then he turned to Rodent. "You saw her."

"Me? I was sawing logs!"

"At the museum. The one you called Old Evil Eyes."

Rodent scowled, trying to remember. "Oh, yeah! The one that wasn't mummified. The one whose mummy had disappeared."

"She's reappeared now," said Peter dismally. "The worst part last night was that I could understand her, inside my head. It was like I was thinking, but in her voice."

"What'd she say?" asked Rodent.

"She said she was the *ka*, the twin, of Tachu and that she wanted one of the cat's bones."

This was too much for Erin. "I read this book of really true stories called *Thirteen Ghosts*, and one's called 'The Curse of the Mummy's Bone.' It's about this woman who stole a mummy's bone from a tomb in Egypt, and when she got home to Scotland, all these horrible, awful things happened to her. Glass broke in the middle of the night and furniture went flying through the air and she died at a really young age."

Peter did not find this terribly hard to believe.

"And remember what I told you about the curse on King Tut's tomb? Well, within one year of the opening of the tomb, practically everybody on the expedition was stone dead."

"Cut it out, Erin! I didn't steal anything from any mummy's tomb!"

"Maybe not, but you've got it now."

Peter groaned.

"Think we should unwrap the mummy?" mused Rodent. "Maybe it's got gold bones or something."

"Forget it!" Peter aimed his pillow at Rodent. "Listen, I don't know how I got involved in all this, but I do know that I'm supposed to keep the mummy away from the *ka* and from any of my so-called friends who want to take it apart!"

"Simmer down. It was just a suggestion."

After simmering down slightly, Peter said, "Could be I'm hallucinating this whole Egyptian thing, and I'm ready for the little men in white coats to come and take me to a rubber room."

Peter hoped that Erin and Rodent would protest this idea, but neither said a word.

"But maybe I'm not hallucinating, and in that case the ghost of this incredibly evil ancient Egyptian is after me and telling me that if I don't get the cat back to Nephia before the full moon, I'll be a man of the past . . . a goner!"

"So give it to her, Pete!" exclaimed Rodent. "You just say, 'Here you are, your royal Evilness, now get out of my life, thank you very much.' "

"I can't. I have to take the cat back to Nephia. I don't know how, but I have to. Tomorrow." Peter sighed. "If the *ka* doesn't come back tonight and take it."

Peter flopped back on his pillows. "Plus," he said slowly, thinking of that crack in the cellar wall, "I've got this awful feeling that if I don't deliver the cat to Nephia, the *ka* will get it and then something awful will happen, something awful for everybody."

AS TACHU'S *SAHU* BLUNDERED THROUGH THE NIGHTMARE landscape, one thought sustained her. *The Potion of Eternity.* Over and over she envisioned her *ka* back on earth retrieving the knucklebone of the Spirit-cat. Again and again she pictured just the way her twin would grind it to powder, sift it with the eleven other ingredients, and boil them under a moonless sky. Countless times did she imagine her *ka* toasting Set with her smoking goblet before drinking the potion down. She could almost smell its bitter aroma, taste the power that would at last belong to Tachu! Her perfect earthly remains were ready and waiting for this moment. Her body was cold as stone now, yes, but once her *ka* had drunk the potion, life and warmth would flow back into her veins. She would burst forth whole again—whole and strong and immortal! Then the throne of Egypt would be hers, not for twenty years or fifty, but forever!

19

THE NEXT TIME MR. HARRING CAME DOWN FROM his study, he shooed Erin and Rodent out of Peter's room. "He's supposed to be sleeping, remember?"

Peter heard Erin and Rodent tiptoe down the stairs. Closing his eyes, he sensed the nearness of Pharaoh and fell immediately back to sleep.

When he woke, it was dark in his room. Something was wrong. He could feel it. Fumbling with the light, he looked under his bed. The space was empty. Pharaoh was gone. And so was the little mummy.

"Pharaoh!" Peter careened down two flights of stairs. "Pharaoh! Where are you?" He catapulted into the kitchen. His parents and sister sat at the table, their soup spoons suspended midair.

"Where's Pharaoh?" cried Peter. "Where is he?"

"Calm down, Peter," said his mother. "How are you feeling?"

"Mom, where's my dog?"

"Think you're ready for some soup?" his mother continued. "It's vegetable."

"Soup, yes, please. Yum, yum," Peter made himself say. "Now what about *Pharaoh*?"

"Rodent's got him," Erin answered.

"Rodent?"

"Your eyes still look a bit feverish." Mrs. Harring placed a steaming bowl in front of her son.

Peter lowered himself into a chair. His head was spinning.

"Rode said he needed to check in at home," Mr. Harring began, "and for some reason Pharaoh seemed determined to go along."

"And wait until you hear what he's doing," said Erin. "It was all my idea."

"He . . . he isn't unwrapping anything, is he?"

"Nope! You'll love what he's doing!"

Rodent must have taken the mummy. That's the only reason Pharaoh would go with him.

Peter pushed his chair away from the table. "I have to call Rodent."

"Finish your supper," said Mrs. Harring. "He said he'd be back around eight. And when you're feeling better, we'll have a discussion about the canyon your dog has dug in our back yard."

Peter blew weakly on the hot soup. Why had Rodent run off with the mummy? Where could he have taken it? Home? To the Met? The Met! Of course. He'd figured out some way to give the cat back to the Princess and by now he'd done it. Peter let out a deep breath. No more voices. No more freaks in the night. No more worrying about becoming a man of the past!

Peter picked up his soup spoon and dug in. He thought that no vegetable soup in the world had ever tasted so good.

After supper, Erin found an old Scrabble board in the parlor and challenged the others to a game. Feeling good for the first time in so long, Peter played well, only losing to Erin by a few points after she managed to spell out ENZYMES on a triple word score.

As he was putting the tiles away, the doorbell rang. For a split second, Peter tensed. Then he felt foolish. His days of hearing voices and seeing evil spirits were over!

"Welcome back, Rode," he heard his mother say.

Peter sped to the door just as Lucinda's beat-up old van was pulling away from the curb and threw his arms around his dog. He hadn't known he could miss him so. "Rode, did you do it? Did you?"

"Aw, Erin snitched. I wanted to surprise you."

"All right!" cried Peter, jubilant. "Who cares about the full moon now? No evil spirit is going to zap me, Rode! You saved my life!"

"Peter, you're not making any sense," said his mother. "I want you back in bed. Rode, you and Erin can keep him company, but try not to get him excited."

The two boys and the dog raced upstairs, with Erin close behind.

As soon as the door was shut, Peter bombarded Rodent with more questions, but his friend merely smiled.

He placed the gym bag he'd been carrying on Peter's bed and unzipped it. "You're gonna love this, Pete." He pulled a small object from the bag and unwound several layers of tissue paper from it. *"Número uno!"*

There, in Rodent's hand, was the cat mummy. He hadn't returned it to Nephia at all!

"Okay, check this out," Rodent said as he unrolled tissue paper from a second object. "Tah-dah! *Número dos!"* In his other hand, Rodent held another cat mummy, identical to the first.

"What's going on?" Peter croaked.

Rodent placed the two mummies side by side on the bed and switched them around like a two-card-monte dealer. "Okay, which is real and which is Memorex?"

"I don't know!"

Erin grinned. "He can't tell!"

"Separated at birth, huh?"

"It was my idea," Erin claimed again.

"But why?" groaned Peter. "Why?"

"Don't you get it?" said Erin.

"It's a forgery, man!" said Rodent. "To fool Evil Eyes! When I told Lucinda what was going to happen to you if you didn't get the real kitty back to the Princess, she was glad to help."

"She believed it?"

"Every word! Lucinda's like that. Of course I had to tell her not to put one of the cat's front legs up in the air and stick a Christmas-tree bulb in its paw for a torch." Looking from one mummy to the other, he chuckled. "The old girl did okay."

"But which is the real one?"

"This one. See?"

Near the cat's feet, a strand of linen was marked with a brown hieroglyph. Peter picked up the second mummy. An identical marking was at its feet, but alongside was something too small for Peter to decipher.

"Lucinda couldn't help herself." Rodent shrugged. "She signed her cat."

"But even if it does fool the *ka* enough so that she rips it open, it'll be empty. No bones."

"Wrong!" said Erin. "I gave Rodent my squirrel skeleton!"

"This little fake-o will fool anybody!" said Rodent.

Peter wanted to believe. Badly. He studied the forgery. It was the same golden color as the real one, and Lucinda had even smudged on dark brown paint in imitation of the pitch that had kept the mummy from rotting away. She had rendered the cat's face perfectly. If the *ka* came back tonight, it might fool her. She might take the false mummy, extract a little squirrel knucklebone, and go back to whatever hell she had come from.

Peter walked over to a window. A strong wind whipped the tree branches against the night sky, hiding, then revealing the nearly full moon. In the changing, dappled light, the hole Pharaoh had dug beneath the sycamore might have been a lunar crater.

Pharaoh joined his master at the window, putting his paws on the sill, and Peter stroked the dog's back thoughtfully. He'd read countless stories in which a hero was given some insurmountable task to perform. The hero never seemed to know exactly *how* he was going to do the impossible deed, but he kept trucking along, being kind to gnarled old grandmothers and trusting in seemingly ordinary things, like a hat or a handful of pebbles. Maybe Peter wasn't the first person that came to mind when the word "hero" was spoken, but somehow he had been chosen, by an ancient power that must know a thing or two, as the man of the future. Thinking this, Peter felt a faint spark of hope rekindle. He still was, after all, Harring the Daring.

By the turn of the twentieth century, many great rulers of Ancient Egypt were sleeping their eternal sleep in the Cairo Museum, and mummies of lesser importance were available for export. And so, one rainy spring morning in 1919, instead of a pharaoh, the Metropolitan Museum of Art received the sister of a king.

The Met's chief curator consulted his pocket watch. He and the six other curators had been standing in this airless room for over three hours and still they were mystified by the body of the ancient Egyptian woman who lay in the bed of sand inside her ornate coffin. Garbed in faded red cloth, she had, by some miraculous means, been preserved whole. Whole! Not a fingernail, not an eyelash was missing. But even more amazing was her skin. Mummy skin was invariably stained and leathery, but hers was downright youthful! Nothing like this had ever been discovered before. Yet, something about the woman—perhaps it was her open, staring eyes—made the curators feel uneasy, and so, after much discussion, they decided not to make any announcement of the acquisition. Instead, they transferred Tachu to a plain black casket, along with the sand that surrounded her, and arranged to put her painted coffin and her amulets on display in the Egyptian Galleries. Then the seven curators swore not to speak of this incident to anyone.

Just before closing time that day, the chief curator sent a message to a colleague at the Museum of Natural History. Early the next week, a horse and wagon were dispatched across town to pick up the unmarked casket.

In an upper room of the Museum of Natural History, two senior anthropologists bent over the ancient cadaver. Between them, they had some fifty-four years of training, including graduate courses in anatomy, physiology, and Egyptology. But neither knew what to make of a body in such condition. Long into the night they argued about probable causes: the properties of the sand in her coffin, the dry air in her tomb, the marked success of some experimental embalming process.

About one thing, and only one, did they agree: the corpse must not be displayed until they could find some explanation for her state of preservation. Then surely newspaper headlines around the world would proclaim their incredible discovery! But until that day they intended to keep the woman's existence a dark secret. When they had finished their research, they returned her to her box and nailed on the lid. And there, on her bed of sand, she rested while their debate continued.

Being men of science, neither of them would have looked to magic as the source of the woman's appearance, even if they had lived out the year. But when the great influenza epidemic of 1919 swept through the country, it claimed them both as victims. Other scientists at the museum were far too busy with their own projects to read through the reams of papers that each man had left behind, and before long their filing cabinets and research materials were put into storage to make room for new scientists hired by the museum. A maintenance worker who helped with the move commented that one of those boxes was devilishly heavy, but he never thought to look inside. And so, after the two anthropologists passed on, not a single soul in the Land of the Living knew what was inside the plain black box that leaned against the storeroom wall.

20

BEFORE HE AND RODENT AND ERIN WENT TO BED that night, Peter slipped Lucinda's forgery out onto the back porch. Then he hid the real Khaibit behind the drawbridge in his headboard and, as additional security, superintended one more art project—the making of dozens of copies of the Eye of Horus. While Erin and Rodent drew, Peter took the pictures and tacked them over every doorway. If Lucinda's handiwork didn't fool the monster, maybe the eye on Pharaoh's collar that had protected him from her curse would protect them in their beds as well.

Thursday morning dawned peacefully, but the sun was high in the sky before Peter awoke. It was after eleven when he bolted out of bed and scuttled frantically, still half-asleep, down the stairs and out to the porch.

"Why didn't somebody wake me up?" he cried. "Where's the fake mummy?"

"She took the bait!" cried Rodent. "Lucinda's mummy fooled her!"

"Don't forget whose idea it was," said Erin.

Peter staggered into the kitchen, thankful to have survived the night, but knowing she'd be back. Hurriedly, he dropped some bread into the toaster, thinking that right after breakfast he and Rodent would catch the subway up to the Met. He didn't know what he was going to do once he got there, but go he must. He buttered the hot toast and took it outside. The three were just finishing their breakfast when Mr. Harring appeared.

"Hi, Dad," said Erin. "Anything new with the TP yet?"

"Very close." Mr. Harring frowned. "Peter, you'd better fill in that hole before somebody falls in and gets hurt."

"I will."

"Now, right away."

"But, Dad, Rode and I have to go up to the Met. We *have* to!"

"For goodness' sake, Peter. You act as if going to an art museum is a matter of life and death."

"It is!" cried Peter. "Trust me, it is!"

"Fill in that hole and then we'll talk. When you're finished eating, get the shovels and get to work."

"But the shovels, they're . . . in the cellar."

Something in his son's expression convinced Mr. Harring that Peter was in earnest about this cellar busi-

ness. "*I'll* get the shovels." His father strode purpose-
fully across the grass. "And you can take it from there."

"No!" Peter jumped up and ran halfway around the
house after his father, but Mr. Harring had already
swung one of the doors open. Quickly, he disappeared
down into the dark space, his footsteps sounding on
the stairs. The light came on. Peter listened for more
footfalls, but heard nothing. He was sure his father been
swallowed by the black hole in the wall. "Dad!" he
called desperately. "Dad!"

"I'm right here, Peter." Mr. Harring, carrying two
heavy gardening spades, came up the steps. "I was not
strangled by King Kong or whatever monster you seem
to think is lurking down there."

Peter nearly collapsed with relief.

Mr. Harring handed him one spade and gave the
second to Rodent. "Sorry, Erin, but there were only
two. Maybe you can convince the boys to take turns."

"No problem," said Erin. "I've got things to do in
the lab."

"And what in the world are these weird drawings
doing over all the place?" Peter's father yanked down
an Eye of Horus that Peter had thumbtacked over the
kitchen door. "Have you kids joined a cult or something?" The screen door slammed behind him.

"What a grouch," observed Erin. "He's really stuck
on the ads."

Rodent worked steadily to help fill in the excavation
beneath the sycamore, and Peter shoveled dirt at an
astonishing pace, but even so, it was nearly three by

the time they finished. Coated with grime, they both needed showers, but the plumber had finally arrived and had turned the household water off while he repaired several leaky pipes. By the time they were cleaned up, it was too late. Getting up to the Met took a good forty-five minutes, if the trains were running on time, and on Thursdays the Met closed at 5:15.

But at dinner that night Peter extracted a promise from his father. "Tomorrow, you can be at the Met the minute they open the doors," he said. "In fact, I'll drop you in a taxi and then loop back downtown to the office. I've called a meeting of my toilet-paper team to wrap up this campaign. We've got to come up with something that old Naper likes, or we're going to lose this account."

"Aren't you boys glad you came with me to the Met?" Mrs. Harring sounded quite pleased with herself. "Why, it's opened you up to a whole new world!"

"You can say that again."

"Be sure to stop by the exhibit of New Guinea bone carvings. I understand they're fabulous." Mrs. Harring turned to her daughter. "Erin, I want Peter and Rode to experience the works of art without anything to distract them, so you can come in to work with me."

"But I want to go, too," whined Erin.

"You know the exotic-bird shop next door to Bookworld?" said Mrs. Harring. "My secretary told me that they just got a new parrot with a six-hundred-word vocabulary."

Erin smiled smugly at the boys. "Who needs your old mummy treasure hunt, anyway?" she said.

That night, Peter thought about booby-trapping the house before he went to bed, but he couldn't figure out how to trip up an evil spirit. In spite of his father's protests, he'd hung more Eye of Horus drawings inside the house, above all the windows and beneath most of the stuffed cat heads. He spent yet another nearly sleepless night feeling that somehow his wakefulness might keep his foe away.

Friday morning finally dawned without a visit from the *ka*. Peter brought Khaibit out of hiding and wrapped the little mummy carefully in an old pillowcase. Then he slipped it into his backpack. He was on his way down the stairs when the awful thought struck. In his mind, when he'd pictured taking the cat to Nephia, Pharaoh had always been beside him. But now that he was actually going, he realized that there was no way he could take a dog into the museum.

After a hurried breakfast, Mr. Harring, dressed this morning in a suit and tie, hustled Peter and Rodent to the door. "Come on. We'll grab a cab on First Avenue and go up the Drive."

Pharaoh sat by the front door, his great yellow eyes following his master's every move. Peter bent down and threw his arms around the dog. "Oh, Pharaoh! How am I going to do this without you?"

"For heaven's sake, Peter," said his father. "You'll only be separated for a few hours. Put the dog out back, and let's hope he's not in a digging mood today."

In the yard, Peter hugged Pharaoh once more, and as he pulled away, the metal disk from his collar slipped into his hand. The source of Pharaoh's power, and now of his own. Peter's fear drained away, replaced by a soaring confidence. Pocketing the disk, he whispered, "Thank you, Pharaoh." Then he closed the gate.

No one spoke as their taxi sped up the FDR Drive, veering from lane to lane, missing other vehicles by mere centimeters. But Peter never flinched, even when they bounced out of a pothole and nearly rammed the rear end of a shiny convertible. He felt certain that the cat mummy had not survived for three thousand years only to be destroyed in a smashup! Every few minutes he put a hand into his pocket to touch his Horus charm. It thrilled him to feel it there, to think that it would magically protect him. Perhaps it even held the power to open Nephia's casket.

The taxi screeched to a halt in front of the museum. "Now, you're just going to the Met, right?" said Mr. Harring. "And to a coffee shop for lunch?" He pulled out his wallet and, while he repeated the litany of city safety rules that Peter had been hearing since he was a tot, counted two tens and five ones and gave them to his son. "That should be plenty. Okay, I'll pick you up right here by the fountain at five sharp. Wish me luck on the toilet paper!" He waved and the taxi sped off.

Peter and Rodent sprinted up the twenty-eight wide stone steps to the museum and walked in. Peter paid a voluntary admission of four dollars each, hoping that the gods of art might take it as an offering and bring him luck with whatever lay ahead. The boys fastened their MMA buttons to their T-shirts and headed for the north entryway, closest to the Egyptian Galleries.

But at the entrance the guard stopped them. "Sorry,

fellas, but you can't bring that pack in here. You'll have to check it."

"But we have to take it in," said Rodent.

The guard's eyebrows went up.

"I mean my friend here keeps his, uh, his medicine in here," Rodent confided in a low voice to the guard. "If we left it behind, well . . ." He stuck his tongue out the side of his mouth and crossed his eyes. "If I were you, I wouldn't want to be responsible for what might happen."

The guard looked skeptically at the well-stuffed pack. "Sorry. Rules are rules."

"Thank you," said Peter, assuming a sickly posture as he walked away to go along with the story.

"Now what?" whispered Rodent.

"Let's try another entrance. There are lots of ways to get into this museum."

But each guard said the same thing. Check the pack.

Peter and Rodent went back outside and sat dejectedly on the museum's stone steps.

"You know," said Rodent, "I bet we're the only people in the world who have ever been stopped from trying to smuggle a priceless art object *into* this museum."

TRIPPING OVER BRAMBLES, DUCKING BENEATH THORNY VINES, the *sahu* tried to ease her suffering by, once again, dreaming of the moment when Tachu would return to life. Ah, yes, she could see it in her mind's eye clearly: Tachu's cheeks regaining their deep copper blush; her lovely hands stirring to push away the lid of her beautiful spell-covered coffin and . . . Oh, brutal fate! Here the dream always fell apart, for the *sahu* could never bear to picture Tachu rising from that ugly black box! Coming to life and finding her gorgeous earthly body in a closet! The *sahu* spat a steady stream of curses as she journeyed on through the endless swamp of the nether world. Archaeologists they called themselves. Indeed! They were no more than tomb robbers. May serpents devour their souls in hell! May tongues of flame lick them forever! She would show their kind. They would be sorry they were ever born. When the prophecy of Maat was fulfilled, when Tachu led the forces of Set out of darkness to inhabit the Land of the Living once more, she would have her revenge on every archaeologist, every museum toady whose work cheated the dead.

Even as she trudged through the slime, evading the snapping teeth of mindless lizards, she mulled over her plan. She would hunt down every living archaeologist, and one by one, she would cut out their pitiful beating hearts! Yes, and before their dying eyes dimmed, they could watch as she swallowed them!

21

FOR NEARLY AN HOUR, RODENT AND PETER SAT on the museum steps racking their brains. Six hours to go. Here they were, so close and yet so far away. There had to be a way to get the cat inside. But how?

A teenage girl in purple cowboy boots jogged up the steps past them. After her came a tall couple with their arms around each other's waists, speaking what Peter guessed might be Swedish. Behind them, a bearded man with a slim ponytail walked toward the art treasures of the world.

"I don't think we can do this, Pete," Rodent said in a discouraged tone. "They make you check everything."

Suddenly Peter sat straight up. "Not everything."

"They do, too! They make you check coats, umbrellas, shopping bags . . ."

Peter shook his head.

Rodent followed Peter's gaze to a woman walking slowly up the steps. On her back, she wore a metal-framed pack in which she carried a sleeping child.

"They don't make you check babies," said Peter.

"Babies? What are you talking about?"

"It might work," Peter said. "If we had a little blanket, maybe a hat, we could wrap the mummy up like a baby and walk right in."

"Aw, what would guys like us be doing walking around with a baby?"

Peter scowled, thinking hard.

"Besides, we don't have any of that baby junk."

"Junk!" Peter popped to his feet. "That's it! Come on!"

Peter charged down the steps. Reluctantly, Rodent followed. He had a bad feeling about this idea of Peter's. A very bad feeling.

Two weeks ago, when his mother had ducked into Junque, Inc., Peter had been so uninterested he hadn't even gone inside. Now his eyes scanned everything in the thrift shop with rapt attention.

"Excuse me," he said to a woman behind a high counter. "Do you have a baby section?"

The woman pointed toward the back of the shop. "And it's all marked fifty percent off right now, sonny."

Peter and Rodent wedged past browsers in the cramped aisles of the men's section, past rumpled suits and tables piled high with wrinkled ties and shirts. They walked through the women's section with its long, silky dresses and balding fur stoles. A mesh playpen signaled the beginning of the baby items. Right away Peter picked up a blue-and-white-striped seersucker pouch with two long sashes and some metal clasps.

"What is that thing?" asked Rodent.

"You know, it's for people to carry their babies on their fronts." Peter turned over the little tag attached to one strap. "Two bucks. Perfect."

Sticking the front pack under one arm, Peter pawed through a table of baby clothes until he found a thin white blanket and a blue hat with a brim. They were fifty cents each.

Rodent did not join in the rummaging.

"That should do it," said Peter, heading back up the aisle. "Let's go."

But Rodent didn't move from the spot where he'd been standing, just outside the baby department. "It's not going to work."

"Why not?"

"The guards will remember you, that's why. First you try to get in with a backpack. An hour later, you try to get in with a front pack. They're for sure going to check out any baby you try to bring into the museum."

But Peter couldn't let go of this idea. He might not get another one. "Maybe we could ask some woman if she'd mind . . ." Peter stopped. A total stranger might think they were trying to smuggle something dangerous into the Met and report them.

"Lucinda'd do it." Rodent sprinted out to the street to call her, but came back a minute later, saying that she didn't answer. "I bet she's there, though. She's probably drilling and didn't hear the phone. We could go down . . ."

"There isn't time, Rode." Peter leaned against a display table. He absently plucked at a scarf, winding it around his finger, and as he pulled, a blank-faced Styrofoam head scooted slightly and toppled over.

"Sonny!" called the woman sitting behind the counter. "Mind the display!"

Peter righted the Styrofoam form and replaced the wig it had been wearing. Pictures in their family photograph album from before he was born showed his mother with a similar 1960s hair style, long and straight. Peter swallowed hard, then lifted the wig off the head again, piling it on top of his other items. He shot a glance over at a rack of women's dresses.

"Oh, no, Pete!" Rodent began backing away from his friend. "I don't even believe what I think you're thinking."

Peter walked over to where a blond woman in sunglasses was browsing through the dresses, one by one. He stood behind her, looking, too.

Rodent grabbed Peter's elbow, pulling him away. "You can't!" he whispered. "You're crazy! You'll . . . you'll end up arrested! It won't work, believe me. For one thing, you don't have enough money to buy a . . . a dress!"

"They're only five dollars," said Peter.

"And for another, they won't fit you! You're too short!"

"Yeah, I know," said Peter. "But you're not."

Rodent remembered a greeting card he'd gotten a couple of years before from his dad's new wife, the only communication he'd ever had from her, when she must have had a single sudden impulse to befriend her husband's son. Inside was a quotation from Robert Louis Stevenson: "A friend is a present which you give yourself." At this moment, as he stood in the dingy little rest room of the Four Brothers Coffee Shop centering a no doubt cootie-infested wig on his head and buttoning up a long, navy-blue silk dress with a pink rosebud pattern, Rodent thought he would like to stick his friend Peter into a big box, wrap it up, and deliver him right to Howie Krieger.

Never much of a money manager, Peter had suddenly shown a ready knack for bargain hunting in Junque, Inc. For only $16.50, he'd bought the front pack, which the woman behind the counter had called a Snugli, the blanket, baby hat, wig, dress, and, to Rodent's great pain and sorrow, a pair of size 10 white patent-leather pumps. Luckily, he didn't have the funds to suggest lipstick or a bra.

Rodent retrieved his MMA button before he wadded his T-shirt up with his jeans and stuck them into the plastic bag from the thrift shop that already held his sneakers. He stuck the button on the lacy collar of his dress—his dress! If only he hadn't dared Peter to touch the mummy, if only he'd kept his big mouth shut for once, then perhaps he'd still be wearing normal clothes. But no. Peter had ranted on and on about how he had to accept some responsibility for the mess he was in, and so, even though he wasn't quite sure he even believed all the weird stuff Peter was into lately, here he was, dressed up like somebody's dotty aunt.

Moaning, he creaked open the bathroom door, which

Peter had sworn on his life to guard, and wobbled out into the coffee shop. The customers continued reading their newspapers.

Peter had ordered and paid for a Coke in obedience to the sign that said REST ROOM FOR CUSTOMERS ONLY. Now, studying Rodent for any telltale signs of boy, he reached into his pocket for a quarter to leave as a tip. Had he not been so concerned about Rodent's appearance, he might have paid more attention to the appearance of the coin he left on the table, which, it turned out, had the outline of an eye etched into it and was worth far more than twenty-five cents.

Peter walked down Eighty-third Street slightly behind Rodent, so no one would take a second look at the odd couple they made. After two blocks, Rodent turned around. "I can't do this! My feet are killing me!" He hobbled over to the steps outside a bookstore, sat down, and pulled off a shoe. "I've got a blister!"

"Here," said Peter, offering the Snugli instead of sympathy. "Put this on."

Peter seemed to be all thumbs as he tried to fasten the straps and buckles to get the thing hooked up the right way, but finally he stepped back and nodded. Then he took the mummy, still in the pillowcase, out of his backpack, wrapped it in the baby blanket, and put the blue, brimmed baby hat on top. He zipped it into Rodent's front pack.

"There," he whispered. "I think you'll make it past the guard."

Rodent stood up, groaning.

"Think of yourself as an undercover cop," Peter advised. "Or a CIA agent."

"Or a truly sick person."

"Thanks, Rode. You could be saving my life."

Rodent just groaned again. Turning, he wobbled off toward the Metropolitan Museum of Art.

ONLY WHEN TACHU'S *KA* WAS WITHIN REACH OF THAT TINY bone which would enable the powers of darkness to control earthly destinies as they never had before, only then did Set command the seven heads of the crocodile to cease the gnashing of their teeth. Only then did he allow Tachu to stumble across an outcropping of rock in the swamp of woe.

The dreaded beast had stopped nipping at her heels! It had turned around and slithered off. The *sahu* could hardly believe her good fortune as she leaned against the rock. Oblivious of its spiky points, she lowered herself to a sitting position, grateful beyond measure to rest. And here she sat, waiting for the victorious return of her twin.

22

PETER FOLLOWED THE STRANGE FIGURE IN THE flowery dress to the Met. Inside, Rodent headed straight for the first entrance they had tried that morning and breezed by the guard without a hitch.

Peter checked his backpack, bulging now with Rodent's clothes, and went to the west entrance, where he, too, walked easily past the guard.

The boys had agreed to meet on a bench beside the Temple of Dendur. On his way, Peter passed Nephia's gallery. It was still roped off to the general public. Her coffin wasn't visible from the doorway, but Peter felt her presence, and it reassured him, until he glimpsed Tachu's mummy case, not far from where he was standing. He hurried away.

Peter found Rodent sitting uncomfortably on a bench opposite the Temple. But before he could reach him, a tall woman with gold-rimmed glasses sat down beside him.

The woman leaned over to Rodent in a confidential way and said, "Girl?"

"What!?" Rodent demanded. Then, remembering, he switched to his high, Ms. McCoy voice. "I mean, what?"

Any other time, this scene would have made Peter roar with laughter, but right now nothing seemed funny.

"Your baby," explained the woman, scooching over even closer on the bench. "Is it a girl?"

"Oh, uh, yes." Rodent smiled sweetly.

The woman reached out a hand. "Could I just take a little peek?"

"No!" Rodent jerked away, his wig sliding slightly as he did. "I mean, no, no," he said in his high voice. "She's sick. Very, very sick."

"Oh, dear! What's the matter? Is she running a temperature?"

"Yes!" Rodent stood up. "Oh, here's my nephew now, the one who promised to take care of the cat . . . uh, little Catrina for me. Please excuse us." He spun away from the woman and made a vicious face at Peter as he hustled him away.

"Get this thing off me," growled Rodent as he headed for the rest room.

But just as he was about to open the door, a guard called loudly. "Ma'am! The ladies' room is just down the hall."

"Oh, my, thank you!"

Since rest rooms were out, Rodent teetered toward Arms and Armor. "I must be out of my mind," he whispered, retreating to a faintly lit side gallery featuring crossbows and motioning frantically for Peter to untie him. When he felt his burden come loose, he thrust it into Peter's arms. "Here. Now hand over the token for the check booth."

"First help me put—" Peter stopped. "Wait a sec. What if I see that nosy woman again? Or what if other people think it's weird for a boy to be running around the Met with a baby?" Peter eyed Rodent hopefully.

"I'm out of here, Pete."

"But couldn't you walk around a little longer, just till I figure out what I'm doing?"

"No way! I've had it with playing mommy to your mummy." He held out his hand. "The token."

"Okay, okay." Peter slapped the small octagonal plastic piece into his friend's palm and Rodent tottered off toward the check booth as fast as his patent-leather pumps would allow.

"When you get changed," Peter called, "meet me on the bench by the entrance." A good place to sit, in case he had to lie low for a while.

Rodent gone, Peter walked slowly over to the short knight's armor. If only he could put the armor on and turn into Harring de Daring for a while, surely he'd figure out a way to get the cat to Nephia. The next best plan seemed to be to hide the mummy and then, when he'd thought of a way, he could retrieve it.

Tucking the bundle under one arm, Peter decided to keep moving. As a city child, he'd been trained to walk the streets with assurance, to stride confidently, to avoid eye contact. Now he applied his lessons in the wide

corridors of the museum. He walked back to the Great
Hall and took a right, past vases and paintings on stone
and carvings, but mostly past sculpted heads that over
the centuries had had their noses knocked off, as if
they'd tangled with some ancient ancestors of Howie
Krieger.

At the end of the hall, he came to the restaurant. Not
many people were around yet, since it was too early
for lunch, so it seemed safe for Peter to sit on a bench
just outside, next to a potted palm. Lost in thought, he
fiddled with a bark chip in the big terra-cotta pot, and
then he noticed that the palm was actually planted in
a smaller plastic container. The small pot had been set
into the wider one, and the difference in diameter filled
in with chips. Peter's eyes assessed the width between
the pots, and then slowly, carefully, he got to work.

With the waiters busy setting up for lunch and with
few guards in this area, Peter was able to dig steadily.
It took him only about ten minutes to scoop out enough
bark chips so that his arm fit into the pot up to his
elbow. He stuck in his bundle, Snugli and all, quickly
brushing chips back to cover it up.

Although he'd made only a temporary arrangement
for the cat, Peter gave a small sigh of relief. Then he
hurried back to the Great Hall and sat down on the
bench where he said he'd meet Rodent.

As Peter sat there, waiting, thinking how to get the
mummy in to Nephia, a shadow slid over him and his
heart nearly stopped. There, glaring down at him, was
the *ka*! As she sensed his fear, her red lips spread into
a cruel smile, and once more her words began drilling
into his skull.

"I offer you one last chance, man of the future! Give me the mummy of Khaibit!" She bent forward, her face coming close to his. *"The real Spirit-cat this time."*

Peter focused his thoughts on a man sitting inside the information booth. The man was losing his hair, his Adam's apple bobbled up and down as he talked to museum visitors, his shirt was the color of taco sauce. Peter thought of anything to keep the *ka* from invading his thoughts and discovering Khaibit's hiding place. To steady his head, he reached into his pocket and fingered what he never doubted was the amulet of Horus.

He was running out of things to think about the information man. Where were the guards? Didn't they think it strange that the museum now had a *living* ancient Egyptian? But as Peter searched the crowd for Rodent, a teenage boy with spiked orange hair and several safety pins sticking through his earlobes rushed by to greet a man wearing a full-length caftan, and he realized that the *ka* looked no more out of place than these two.

Where was Rodent?

The woman in red gripped Peter's mind once more. Unresisting, he got to his feet and followed her past a guard at the north entrance. She was leading him toward the room where her own casket was displayed, where Nephia's coffin lay. He didn't know why exactly, but he didn't want the *ka* to get anywhere near Nephia. As they passed a wide stairway leading to the floor below, Peter wrenched away from the *ka* and ran down. She would follow, that was certain, but at least this might buy him a few seconds.

The stairway ended outside the entrance to the Costume Institute. A sign announced the title of this season's exhibit: STYLES OF THE IMMORTAL MONARCHS.

Peter dashed into the gallery. The lights were low here. Not many people were around, just a tour group at the far end of the first room. He hoped coming to this dim, less populated gallery hadn't been a mistake. Then, he felt the *ka*'s revolting grip once more and there she was beside him.

He expected her to lead him up the stairs again, but she merely stood by his side, as if transfixed by what she saw: a mannequin dressed in white linen pleated at the waist, with a wide blue beaded collar. On her head rested a golden crown that appeared to be a bird with its wings spread down, fitting over her ears. A sign identified the figure as Queen Nefertiti.

The *ka* stared in silence for a few seconds and then Peter heard her voice. *"This was a Queen of Egypt?"*

"That's what it says."

"She was after the time of Tachu. Do you think her very beautiful?"

Peter shrugged as he saw something that he did think very beautiful—the dog by Nefertiti's side. It could have been Pharaoh's twin, his *ka*. Lettering on the information card read *The Royal Dog of Egypt*. Even in his agony, Peter smiled, thinking how he would enjoy telling Erin, if he lived long enough, that the "mutt" he'd found in the taxi was, in reality, the most ancient of pedigreed dogs.

Still staring at Nefertiti, the *ka* filled Peter's head with angry muttering. She took a step toward the next mannequin, and her frown deepened.

Hoping to add to her displeasure, Peter thought: "That's Cleopatra, the most famous Queen of Egypt."

"The most famous," the *ka* repeated. Then she whirled on Peter. *"Do you know why the statue of Tachu is missing? Why it is not here among the immortal monarchs?"*

Peter shook his head.

"Because of that dreadful girl! That horse-loving fool! If not for her, Tachu would have been more than Queen! Tachu would have been Pharaoh!"

Peter's head throbbed with this tirade and he realized he could see Queen Cleopatra right through the *ka*. In her fury, every part of her except the small blue pouch at her throat was dematerializing. But again she read his thoughts and, closing her eyes, she clasped the pouch. At once, she became solid. Her long fingers kneaded the turquoise leather. *"These queens did not rule Egypt as Pharaoh! Not as Pharaoh!"*

Not as Pharaoh. These words triggered some vague memory for Peter. What was it? And suddenly he knew.

"Pharaoh!" he whispered, and for once he was not calling his dog.

THE MAN OF THE FUTURE WAS IN TERRIBLE DANGER! NEPHIA
had just one chance left to speak. She must speak now
and help him! Perhaps she should say: *Beware the eyes
that spit fire!* But what good would that do? He had lost
the protection of the Horus charm, and without it, he
could not shield himself from her deadly gaze should
she decide to use it.

Ah! Maybe this: *Recite now the supplication to Isis,
divine mother, mistress of charms and enchantments!*
But did he know the long prayer? She, in her twelve
years upon the earth, had barely managed to memorize
the first portion.

> *O Queen of the gods,*
> *Save us all from evil demons,*
> *Save us from the serpent's tooth,*
> *Save us from . . .*

From what? Oh, why had she paid so little heed to her father's teachings? So much depended upon her words! The wrong ones could ruin everything, yet the right ones seemed to elude her. She must think. Think! But she was thinking so hard already that, even in paradise, her head was beginning to ache, not unlike her twentieth-century champion's head at this very moment.

23

WRENCHING OUT OF THE *KA*'S GRIP ONCE MORE, Peter bolted from her side and charged up the steps, nearly knocking a woman to the floor. At the top of the staircase, he forced himself to a rapid walk so as not to attract attention. Through the Egyptian Galleries he sped, searching for the second entrance to the gallery just beyond Nephia's. At last he stopped, panting for breath, in front of four immense stone statues of a seated Pharaoh.

Only half a dozen other people were in this gallery. Each had a tape recorder strapped across one shoulder and wore earphones. Not one of them looked up just seconds later when the *ka* slithered into the room.

Peter wasted no time in gathering his thoughts. "When you have statues like these made of you, the world will always know who you are. Your name will be in history books. It's a way of being immortal, of living forever."

The *ka*'s narrowed eyes left Peter's face and flickered up to an enormous stone face.

"Let me introduce you to Hat-shep-sut." Peter thought the long name carefully. "She was Pharaoh of Egypt."

The flood of the *ka*'s angry muttering slowed to a trickle. She stared up at the statue, growing translucent again.

"Hatshepsut reigned for more than twenty years." He strained to remember what else he'd heard the guide say about her, what facts Erin had spouted. "Hatshepsut was the highest power in the world, the Pharaoh."

The *ka*'s diaphanous body grew rigid. She held her arms straight against her sides, her hands clenched in fists. *"NO!"* she shrieked in a strangled voice that made Peter dizzy with pain. *"It should be Tachu!"*

The *ka* was more ghostly than ever. Peter whipped his head around to see if anyone was looking at this strange, disintegrating figure, but the group with the earphones was attending only to the works of art.

His plan seemed to be working, but he had to press on, to keep goading her until she faded entirely out of this world.

"Not Tachu," Peter thought firmly. "Tachu never did anything important. Her brother was Pharaoh. Amenhut's statue is right there, by that doorway. Can you see it?"

The *ka*'s eyes bulged with hatred. *"Amenhut was nothing but a mewling, poetry-scrawling scribe! He ignored the Land of Egypt! He should have been forgotten while he yet lived! The* ka *of Tachu spits on the weakling!"*

Peter stepped back, not wanting to be in the way in case she carried out her threat.

"And on his daughter! Curses on her head!" The *ka* glared menacingly at Peter, without seeming to see him. Trembling with the unfairness of it all, she addressed the largest of Hatshepsut's statues. *"Tachu should sit where you sit! TACHU!"*

She was sheer as a ghost.

"All that's left of Tachu is an empty mummy case." Peter aimed to finish her off. "The world has forgotten Tachu."

"Why did Tachu bother—with a chariot driver—with such an elaborate plan?" wailed the *ka*. She raised a fist to the heavens. *"Better to have used . . ."* The voice inside Peter's head, like the rest of the *ka*, was fading: *". . . poison!"*

As the word "poison" sounded in his head, Peter could barely see the outline of the *ka*. The turquoise pouch seemed to float in midair. Yes, she was disappearing from this world and returning, he hoped, to her misery of eternal wandering.

But as she lowered her gossamer fist, her fingers brushed against the turquoise pouch at her throat, and before Peter had time to realize what was happening, she had wrapped her hand around it. Immediately she stood before him again, solid and whole. Sparks flew from her eyes. One or two hit Peter, stinging his bare arms. Her chest heaving, panting for breath, the *ka* whirled on Peter. *"GIVE ME THE MUMMY OF KHAIBIT! TACHU WILL BE IMMORTAL!"*

Now not only the voice pressed into Peter's head, but the *ka*'s frigid grasp, her rotting scent, her iron will.

Peter's stomach churned. Dots of light and shadow danced dizzily before his eyes as the *ka*'s words penetrated his skull. And then the pain he could not endure eased a bit. Soothing words took its place, words that told him this was a battle he could not win. Comforting words advised him to give up. What business of his was it, anyway, whether some old mummy got her cat back? What difference did it make if he told good *ka*, sweet *ka*, where the mummy was? She would find it in the end, wouldn't she? And how much easier, so much easier, to do it now.

The *ka* drew away a little, hovering expectantly, waiting for Peter's response.

How he wanted to tell! To be finished with this whole business! But a feeling deep inside him, deeper than the *ka*'s words had penetrated, held on. Peter shook his head. No.

The pain stabbed again as the *ka* grew taller, more menacing than ever. *"GIVE ME THE MUMMY NOW! DO NOT DARE TO DISOBEY THE WISHES OF TACHU! DO NOT DARE!*

DARE!

DARE!

DARE!"

As the word echoed in Peter's skull, something familiar slid down his spine. A chill, a thrill. Did somebody say *dare*?

Inside his head, Peter slammed a door. If he tried with all his might, maybe he could keep it closed, keep the *ka* out of at least part of his thoughts. And in this small space he could think for himself, for now it was up to him, Harring the Daring, Future Man, to keep this dark power from establishing itself in the world once more.

"I hid the mummy," thought Peter, struggling to keep the rest of his mind a blank.

"*TAKE ME TO IT NOW!*" the *ka* demanded.

Peter turned from the statues of Hatshepsut and sped off, hoping to avoid the grip of his enemy. He could feel her close, hovering behind him. Down long corridors she followed. He didn't know where he was going, but at least he was in the lead.

At last, he reached a huge stone sarcophgus, its lid propped open by thick metal braces. Beside it stood two uniformed guards.

"The mummy's in there." Peter tilted his head in the direction of the sarcophagus.

For one horrible moment, Peter was afraid that, like Superman, the *ka* had X-ray vision; that she had only to look through the sarcophagus wall to know that he was lying. But she grasped the edge of the great coffin and disappeared inside.

His heart beating hard, Peter turned, expectant, to the guards, those guards who came running if anyone mistakenly passed within inches of a work of art. But now they simply ignored a woman in a bright red dress climbing into a sarcophagus. And suddenly Peter understood. They don't see her!

The *ka* was sliding out of the sarcophagus now, sliding toward him. Peter stumbled backward, digging into his pocket. He had saved the Eye of Horus as a last resort. Now its time had come. His fingers closed around the cool metal circle. He pulled it out of his pocket and thrust it at the *ka*.

The monster hesitated. Peter saw the puzzled look on her face. It was working! It was keeping her away! But . . . what was this? To his horror, Peter saw, between the thumb and first finger of his right hand, not the golden disk from Pharaoh's collar! Not the Eye of Horus! But the silvery profile of George Washington! To protect himself from an evil Egyptian sorceress, Peter was holding out a genuine American quarter.

Quick as a flash, a hand reached out to grasp the turquoise pouch, but this time the hand was not the *ka*'s. Without stopping to think, Peter had grabbed the ancient leather and yanked with all his might. A shock went through his palm. The pain in his head had been nothing. This was unimaginable! Like gripping freezing fire! Icy vapors burned into his flesh. As he heard a sound like the snapping of an icicle, he tumbled to the floor.

"Son?" A guard stood over him. "Are you all right, son?"

"Think so," Peter managed, getting to his knees. The pouch was like a live coal in his hand. Inside his head, the *ka*'s venomous curses thundered. He wanted nothing more than to throw the thing to the floor. Gritting his teeth, he held on and walked unsteadily away from the guard, not daring to look back.

Taking short, gasping breaths, Peter steered his feet toward the Temple. He could feel the *ka* behind him, drilling her way into his mind with a piercing wail. As he went, he struggled to loosen the golden threads that held the mouth of the pouch together. Icy needles stabbed into his fingers as he worked to untie knots that surely were as strong as the day they had been tied thousands of years before.

Reaching the Temple entrance, Peter veered toward a family of obvious out-of-towners, who politely held the door open for him. By the reflecting pool, he stumbled. The fire in his hand, the icy claw squeezing his head. It was too much. And now, like some genie escaped from a bottle, the *ka*'s essence surrounded him, a gaseous, poisonous thing. Each breath he took brought an evil reek through his nostrils, making Tachu a part of him.

Reeling beneath the Temple of Dendur, Peter desperately plucked at the pouch strings. He held his breath and silently cried. *Help me!* And then his lips began to move: *O Queen of the gods, save us all from evil demons, save us from the serpent's tooth, save us from the worm, eater of souls, save us when we say your sacred name, O Isis!* Where the words came from he knew not, but as he uttered this strange invocation, he felt the strings give way. He dug a finger into the tiny opening at the neck of the pouch and wiggled it bigger. And then, just as he thought his lungs would burst, just as he felt that he could bear the pain no longer, he tilted the pouch. Half a second before his eyes rolled back in his head, he saw fine silvery grains spilling out into the pool.

Around him and inside him, horrible screams exploded and Peter knew his skull was splitting. And then nothing. Silence. He took in a ragged gasp of air. It was fresh, untainted. The throbbing in his hand stopped. He looked around and saw no towering fiend, no ghostly red presence. Rather, people walked by him, on their way to view the Temple. Regular, ordinary New York City people, hardly noticing a boy who, they must think, had tripped over his own feet as he threw a wishing penny into the pool.

SITTING ON THE COLD ROCK, TACHU'S *SAHU* FELT A JOLT AS her *ka* spirit returned. Instantly she understood. There would be no smoldering cup of potion, no rebirth of her beautiful earthly form, so lovingly preserved. Uttering a moan of despair, Tachu pushed herself from the rock and took a few jagged steps. She had no destination, no plan. Her wandering, she knew, would be eternal. She only listened for the sound of gnashing teeth that she felt sure would soon begin behind her.

Imagine her surprise then, when out of the swirling dark stepped Anubis, his jackal eyes upon her. He stretched out his hand to her. Ah, of course. It was her heart he had come for, the fountain of all her thoughts both good and evil. Had there been many good ones, she wondered as the *ab* spirit slid away from her? No, not many.

Her heart was in the palm of Anubis now. And at his side, like a hound at the side of its master, sat the Gobbler. Merciful fate, thought Tachu. No longer would she have to flee the beast with seven heads. No longer would she fear the teeth as sharp as knives. She felt only a slight pang as she realized that her earthly body, so captivating still inside that horrid black box, would turn at once to dust. Yet she watched with something akin to gladness as Anubis tossed her stony heart into the air, watched with fleeting joy as it somersaulted slowly into the Gobbler's jaws, and . . . *pif!*

24

A SCRAP OF BLUE FLOATED, HARDLY NOTICEABLE, by the far edge of the reflecting pool. Tiny sparks of light glinted off the grains of the powder on the pool's bottom. From them, small bubbles rose to the water's surface, where they noiselessly popped. So much for the Potion of Eternity.

Peter felt drained yet exhilarated. And it was a good thing, for Harring the Daring, Future Man, had yet another impossible deed to do. Even though he still had no plan for accomplishing it, his recent victory gave him hope.

Peter returned to the Great Hall. He waited a few minutes, but when no Rodent appeared, he went back to the restaurant. Now the area teemed with long lines of people waiting to be seated and he had to loiter for what seemed like an eternity before a place on the bench beside the palm became vacant. After he sat down, he had to remove the bark chips over the

mummy slowly, picking up a few at a time and trans-
ferring them to another pot, all the while trying to re-
main inconspicuous. And even when he could touch
the mummy with his fingertips, he had to wait to grab
it until the long line of museum visitors waiting for
lunch were finally shown to their tables.

As the last diners, a pair of thin women dressed in
navy blue, followed the maître d' down the steps to the
restaurant, Peter whisked the bundle out of the pot,
held it close to his body, and followed the signs to the
nearest men's room. There, inside a stall, Peter struggled
to put on the front pack. It buckled over the shoulders,
he remembered, and tied in the back, just below his
waist. At last, feeling that he had done his best with
the carrier, he zipped in the cat and placed the little
blue hat on its head. Taking a deep breath, Peter walked
out of the stall.

Time was not on his side. He had to get the cat to
Nephia before an alert guard got to him. Boldly, he
walked the length of the museum once more. Reaching
the velvet rope that blocked entry to the gallery, he
offered his most innocent smile to the nearest guard,
who happened to be the one with the trim little mustache, the one who had come running just after he'd
kissed Nephia. The guard stared at the Snugli.

"My brother," Peter said, patting the bottom of the
pack and opening his brown eyes wide. "He's such a
big, heavy baby that my mom gets tired sometimes, so
I help her out when I can."

"Very nice."

Peter didn't think the guard recognized him. "What

I wanted to ask was whether those kids in there are with some special group or whether anyone can go in?"

"What kids?"

Peter stuck a thumb in the direction of the Temple. "The ones wading in the pool in there."

"Wading?" Now the guard opened his eyes wide.

"Splashing around, having a great time," Peter went on. "I didn't see any guards in there to ask, so I came out here, because if it's okay, I wouldn't mind—"

"Excuse me." The guard walked quickly to a metal box in the wall, opened it, and picked up a phone receiver. He said a few fast words into it and then sped off. More guards materialized from the opposite end of the gallery. They all hurried to the Temple.

Peter ducked under the rope and ran silently to Nephia. His head tingled now as he looked down at her mummy case, at her small smile. He knelt down beside the casket and bowed. "I have brought you the treasure of your soul," he whispered to Nephia's earthly remains. He waited, hoping to receive some instruction, some message that might tell him what to do. But none came, and he knew the guards would be back any second. With both hands, Peter took hold of the casket lid. Remembering what the guide had said about it being stuck fast, he gave his mightiest pull and nearly toppled over backward as the lid slipped off. Quietly, he placed it on the floor.

There was the mummy of Nephia, wrapped in linen and lying on her side in the case. Peter hoped she could see out through the Eye of Horus painted on her coffin, see him, her man of the future.

Footsteps in the adjoining gallery snapped Peter's attention back to the job at hand. Quickly, he unzipped the Snugli and pulled out Khaibit. He peeled off the blanket and the pillowcase, then laid the little cat gently beside Nephia. He had no trouble finding the spot where it belonged, nestled up against the chest of his mistress. The cat and the Princess fit together like long-separated pieces of a puzzle. As he put the two together, Peter felt more than heard a deep and satisfied sigh.

He picked up the coffin lid. "Goodbye, Nephia," he whispered, putting it on. To make sure that it was on straight, Peter tried to jiggle it, but the lid didn't budge. Peter pulled up on it again, hard, but the lid was firmly attached to the base of the casket.

Peter allowed himself a sigh now, as he wadded the blanket and pillowcase back into the Snugli and stuck the hat on top. He'd done it. He'd really done it! He bowed again to the Princess, then turned and walked swiftly out of the gallery in the opposite direction from which he had come.

As he bent to duck beneath the rope, another guard called to him, "Hey! You can't go in there!"

"Oops!" he said. "Thanks for telling me."

Peter walked out into the Great Hall and at once spotted Rodent, dressed like Rodent again.

"Pete!" he cried. "I've been looking all over this place for you."

Peter couldn't find his voice. His knees felt suddenly shaky. He sat down on the bench surrounding the plantings by the north entrance.

"So spill, Pete. Is it mission accomplished?"

Peter nodded. "I'll tell you every detail, but right now I'm weak with hunger. What time is it, anyway?"

Rodent looked at his watch. "A little after four."

"Come on, let's see what we can find to eat."

At the bottom of the Met's stone steps, Peter wordlessly handed the Snugli and its contents to a young woman pushing a baby carriage. Then he pulled what money he had left from his pocket. "I've only got a buck and"—he frowned down at the coin in his hand—"a quarter."

"Sounds like pretzel time," said Rodent. "There's a vendor right behind the museum, in the park."

Standing beside the pretzel cart, Rodent split the salty twist in two and handed half to Peter, who was again lost in thought.

"Now what?" said Rodent.

"I had the disk from Pharaoh's collar in my pocket," said Peter, "but I think I must have left it on the table in that coffee shop when—"

Before he could finish his thought, Peter heard a voice call out his name—a voice from the not so distant past.

"Well, if it isn't Harring the Daring."

Behind him stood Howie Krieger.

"And good ol' Ratface," said Howie.

This time Rodent did not correct him. He was too busy thanking his lucky stars that he hadn't run into Howie when he'd been wearing a dress.

As usual, a pair of thugs flanked Howie. "How is the little daredevil?" Howie squeezed Peter's upper arm with his thumb and first finger. "Oooo-eeee! Have you been lifting weights?"

His buddies laughed and slapped one another on the shoulder.

Peter's mind was a blank. He didn't even think about his nose and how much it was going to hurt.

"Guess it's time for the dare of the day," crooned Howie. "I dare you to punch me in the smeller."

Rodent put his hands over his eyes. "I can't watch!"

And so it was that Rodent didn't see Peter step forward, close to Howie; didn't see him with an expression so fierce that the big bully backed away. The first Rodent knew of what was happening was when he heard Peter shouting.

"The dare stuff is over, got it, Howie?"

"Huh?"

"Over! Finished! Done!"

"Wha . . . ?"

Peter was moving forward again, and a flabbergasted Howie was in retreat. "And if I ever see you torturing any more little kids, you're gonna be sorry."

"Me?" Howie's voice squeaked up on the word. He took another step back, into a chain-link fence.

"You." Peter stabbed a finger at Howie's chest. Then he turned abruptly and stomped down the path toward Fifth Avenue. Rodent scampered after him, but not before hearing one of Howie's buddies say, "Geez, Howie. You sure that was the same kid?"

A few minutes after five, a taxi pulled up in front of the Met and Mr. Harring leaned out, waving. The boys joined him in the back seat.

"Well, tonight we celebrate," Mr. Harring said by

way of a greeting. "We got the toilet-paper campaign rolling, and, Peter, you are partly responsible."

"Me?"

"You and that strange dream you had, about the mummies. Picture a pair of mummies, all white, sitting on these big thrones made out of Naper Toilet Paper rolls. Are you ready for the slogan?" Mr. Harring cleared his throat. " 'It's wrapped just right and each roll lasts an eternity.' Great, isn't it?"

"Super, Dad."

"Really brilliant," said Rodent.

"Yes," admitted Mr. Harring. "It is." After a short pause, he added, "So, how was your day at the Met?"

"Not bad," said Rodent.

"Tell me all about it. What did you do?"

"Oh, you know, Dad," said Peter. "Just the usual things you do at a museum."

AMENHUT SITS ON A THRONE OF IRON. ITS ARMS ARE CARVED with the faces of lions; its legs, with the hooves of a bull. In front of him, his writing table is equipped with sheets of heavenly papyri, flawless reed pens, and a jar of celestial ink. Dressed in white linen and sandals, he wears a crown from the gods. He has just eaten the bread of Amen-Ra and drunk the beer of everlasting-ness. Now Amenhut sits on his throne and looks out at the clear lake in the Field of Peace.

The Pharaoh's seven spirits reside in him contentedly. He is one with the gods now; he eats what the gods eat and drinks what they drink.

As Amenhut dips a pen into the ink, he is thoughtful. It is not as easy as he had thought, in this serenity, to compose a poem. Things are perfect. The sky is blue, the sun is shining, a fragrant breeze blows from the north. Too perfect. Where is the storm cloud, the ten-sion, that a fine poem requires? It is deep in his memory.

He shall have to think back over the centuries in order to write.

The Pharaoh closes his eyes. Perhaps he will write of Nephia, his lovely girl, now contented herself in the Fields of Peace. He could tell of her battle against the forces of evil to regain Khaibit, her beloved spirit companion.

Ah, but the sun is blissfully warm. Perhaps the Pharaoh will dangle his feet in the lake as he thinks about his poem. And what a fine thing a little nap would be. Perhaps when he awakens . . . perhaps after that . . . or perhaps tomorrow . . . for, in truth, when all eternity stretches before one, there is no particular need to hurry.

25

"I'D BETTER CHECK IN WITH LUCINDA," RODENT explained, asking Mr. Harring to have the taxi driver drop him off at his place on the way down to Third Street. To Peter, he added, "I hung out in the Met's gift shop while I was waiting for you, and I think Lucinda could make a bundle selling mummy sculptures in there. Who knows? Maybe they'd even go for the Liberties. And besides"—he gave Peter a funny half smile—"I'm starving for some Chinese food."

When the taxi pulled up in front of the Coffin house, Peter jumped out. "Pharaoh!" he called, opening the front gate. "Pharaoh!" But no dog came running to meet him.

While Mr. Harring went on into the house, Peter ran into the back yard, calling. When he got no response, he sprinted upstairs and looked under his bed. No Pharaoh. He ran to the lab, checked in every spot where he'd ever seen his dog sleeping. They were all empty.

"Dad," said Peter, coming into the kitchen, "have you seen Pharaoh?"

"Not in here."

Still calling, Peter walked out to the sycamore, treading on the freshly spaded earth. No dog. Going around the side of the house, he opened the cellar doors. "Pharaoh?"

Forgetting his fear, he ran down the stairs, calling all the while. But only his own voice echoed in the empty, cavelike space. Walking back to the stairs, Peter turned, dreading to see the rip in the wall. A jagged crack ran from ceiling to floor, but that was all. An old crack in an old wall. Could he have imagined the way it was before?

Peter stepped into the yard. His sister had arrived home and was sitting on the back porch, sorting feathers. "Hey, Erin, have you seen Pharaoh?"

"You know what? I met an African gray parrot today who can talk better than most people. You can't find Pharaoh?"

And suddenly Peter knew. Of course no one had seen Pharaoh. He was gone. Nephia had sent him to help get the mummy and now the job was done. Now Pharaoh could return to wherever it was he'd come from in the first place. Of course, Pharaoh hadn't been a real dog. He'd known that all along. But still—he wished he'd been able to say goodbye.

"What happened at the Met?" asked Erin. "Did the evil mummy show up?"

Her brother shrugged. "I'll tell you later." And from

the expression on his face, even Erin knew better than to ask anymore.

Peter walked around the house, calling listlessly, while his father told his mother every detail of the new Naper campaign, and his sister organized her new collection. But when he went in to dinner, just before dark, no dog had showed up.

Mrs. Harring had made a chicken-and-rice dish that was usually Peter's favorite, but tonight he had no appetite. All his good feelings had fled, replaced by a deep sadness.

"Did you hear Bones and the rest of those tattooed hoodlums brawling last night? That rival gang, the Nomads, biked in from the Coast around 2 a.m. and—" Mr. Harring was cut off by the doorbell ringing. "Hold your horses, I'm coming."

"It's probably the carpenters." Mrs. Harring sighed. "Right in the middle of dinner."

Mr. Harring came back to the table looking puzzled and holding a yellow envelope. "A telegram from . . ." He tore the envelope open and scanned the message. "Holy Toledo!"

"Spill, Dad," said Erin.

"KATHRYN COFFIN'S CLOSEST RELATIVE ANOTHER HARRING STOP," the wrong Mr. Harring read. "KINDLY VACATE PREMISES BY TUESDAY STOP WILL COVER MOVING EXPENSES AND THEN SOME STOP DEEPEST APOLOGIES JARVIS SCRULL."

"But what about my laboratory?" wailed Erin. "I can't live without my laboratory!"

"I think you'll survive," said her mother.

Erin squeezed out a few more tears before she added, "If I can't have a lab, can I at least get that parrot?"

"We'll see, we'll see. Byron, I'll bet the closest relative is Cousin Rufus."

"How come you don't like Cousin Rufus, Mom?" asked Erin.

"Well, you know that your father's entire family are redheads, and Cousin Rufus came to our wedding all the way from Cincinnati and told me that he objected to our marriage on the grounds that I am a brunette." Mrs. Harring huffed disdainfully. "He said that your father showed a callous disregard for his genes."

"Oh, Cincinnati Red's a big joker," Mr. Harring chuckled.

Mrs. Harring was not at all amused. "Even if Cousin Rufus is nothing but a red Harring, he's welcome to this house. Am I the only one who misses our sunny little apartment? This house is just so . . . well, old and dark and big, and it needs so much work. Don't you agree, Byron?"

Mr. Harring nodded. "Absolutely. But I thought you were wild about this place."

"Can we take some of the cat heads with us?" asked Erin.

Mrs. Harring shook her head. "I hope never to set eyes on another mounted head as long as I live. Why, it's a crime that these magnificent animals were killed just to decorate a wall."

The spell is broken, thought Peter. *It's over.*

"And it's a good thing that professor isn't in our apartment yet," Mrs. Harring went on. "I'll phone him right after dinner and tell him it isn't available after all, and if I notify the movers . . ."

"Just a minute, Jean," interrupted Mr. Harring. "Peter, can you make that dog of yours stop barking? I can't hear a thing you're saying."

Peter frowned and then heard the barking himself. "It's not Pharaoh, Dad. He doesn't bark, remember? And besides, I think he's . . . run away."

"Oh no, Peter!" exclaimed Mrs. Harring. "How could he have gotten out of the yard?"

"I don't know, but he's not here."

The barking outside grew louder.

"Maybe you should make some signs to put around the neighborhood," suggested his mother.

"Offer a reward," added his sister. "I'll chip in."

"Thanks, Erin, but I don't think it'll help."

"If he doesn't come back, you can get another dog. You certainly showed that you were responsible in taking care of Pharaoh, didn't he, Byron?"

"Very responsible. Why, your mother and I never had to remind you about walking him or feeding him. But how about a smaller dog, this time?"

"I don't want another dog."

"Listen," said Mr. Harring, "I can hardly enjoy this meal for all the noise."

Still chewing disinterestedly on a drumstick, Peter got up from the table to investigate.

"Those pants you have on are getting too short," his mother observed as he walked to the front door. "Why, I believe you've grown a couple of inches."

Ordinarily, Peter would have welcomed this news, but now it hardly mattered. The full moon lit his way down the steps. As he opened the front gate, a dog bounded in, jumping up, barking, yipping, running crazily in a circle around him, then rolling over on his back, wriggling with happiness on the ground, wildly wagging his tail.

"Come here, dog," called Peter. "Let me take a look at you."

The dog gave a happy whine and righted itself. It leaped up on Peter and its wide, soft tongue began kissing his neck, his cheeks, his hair. Peter laughed. "Cut it out, dog!"

The dog ran in another frantic circle around Peter and then jumped up on him again, this time sniffing the piece of chicken, nipping at it.

"Hey, are you hungry?" In the moonlight, Peter saw a white patch on the dog's chest. He thought its head came up to his elbow, the way Pharaoh's had done, but it was jumping around so much it was hard to tell. No, this was not a solemn dog. There was no golden collar around its neck, but it did have large, pointed ears. "Pharaoh?" he whispered. "Pharaoh?"

At the sound of the name, the dog sat at attention, his deep gold eyes riveted on Peter. Yes, they were the same eyes that he had looked into so many times before, but now there was something different about them, something loving and begging and completely doggy.

"Whooopie!" Peter threw his arms around Pharaoh's neck. "I've got you back!" Hugging the dog tight, he cried, "Oh, thank you, Nephia, wherever you are!"

And as the first star of the evening winked in the moonlit sky, Peter thought he heard that small musical voice ringing one last time inside his head. *"Thank you, man of the future!"*